MÉLANIE

Mélanie

by

Alix Taylor

Illustrated by
SUSANNE SUBA

constable

LONDON
PUBLISHED BY
Constable and Company Ltd
10–12 ORANGE STREET, W.C.2

INDIA
Orient Longmans Private Ltd
BOMBAY   CALCUTTA   MADRAS   NEW DELHI

CANADA
Longmans, Green and Company
TORONTO

SOUTHERN AFRICA
Longmans Southern Africa (Pty) Ltd
CAPE TOWN   JOHANNESBURG   SALISBURY

EAST AFRICA
Longmans, Green and Company
NAIROBI

AUSTRALIA
Thomas C. Lothian
SYDNEY   ADELAIDE   MELBOURNE
BRISBANE   AUCKLAND (N.Z.)

MADE AND PRINTED IN GREAT BRITAIN BY
THE GARDEN CITY PRESS LIMITED
LETCHWORTH, HERTFORDSHIRE

For the Cushions—

MIMI AND BRIE
LILYON AND FORBES

her scooter, waited for Luc and Toinon to race her round the
lawn. But if her foot was firmly planted in readiness, her head
was in the clouds, her mind far away from the realities of the
Luxembourg Gardens where she now stood. She was seeing
herself a victorious cyclist, a wreath of laurels crowning her long
straight hair, while she accepted the accolade of the French
government from a representative, resplendent in high hat and
tails. She was startled from this reverie by the sound of Nurse's
voice, calling in her most strident tone, "Claude, come back!"

She looked up to see her three-year-old brother running in
wild circles on the forbidden grass. The large oval lawn around
which people could sit or walk, but over which none was allowed
to trespass under threat of fine or imprisonment, had a small
round flower-bed in its centre, out of reach of dogs who did not
read and children without fear. And there was Claude, running
as though possessed, round and round the mound of carefully
planted earth, trampling the dark green grass as if it were a tun
of grapes.

Again Nurse called, "Claude!" But the speeding demon was
not listening. After her initial surprise, Mélanie was overcome
by a desire to laugh. Claude, his short legs flying out sideways,
his curly hair blown high above his head, looked so like a mech-
anical toy gone out of control, that she almost forgot the serious
aspects of the deed. Her silent laughter was cut short by the
rising impatience in Nurse's voice. "Claude, come back at once!"

Suddenly Luc shot past his sisters and dashed across the lawn.

He grabbed his brother's hand but, instead of leading him off the grass, he took him on another dizzy round about the flower-bed. Claude was laughing hysterically, but Luc, for all of his seven years, had the determined expression of one performing an unpleasant but necessary task. Just then a park guard appeared on the path. The children knew him well. It was Monsieur Guitard. His sudden apparition made Mélanie so nervous that she did not look into his pink round face nor notice, as she had many times before, how, inflated by wine and cheese, he seemed always about to burst the impressive array of brass buttons which adorned his uniform. With his hands behind his back, he stood and gazed in silence at the two boys still running in circles. By now, several people had gathered on the edge of the grass to watch the show.

"Luc! The guard!" Mélanie screamed in warning. M. Guitard put his whistle to his lips and blew. The shrill sound made Mélanie wince. Her sister, Toinon, slipped a cold hand into hers. At the sound of the whistle, Luc and Claude stopped dead. Then slowly, very slowly, they walked across the lawn towards the onlookers. As soon as they were on the path, Nurse raised her hand, but Luc pulled his brother towards him, and it flailed the air. A huge grin lit up M. Guitard's face, and Nurse foolishly smiled back at him. Relieved at having the attention drawn away from them, the four children were quick to lengthen the distance between the guard and themselves. A few feet away they came to a standstill. There, Luc lifted his hand, just as Nurse had done, and struck Claude across the face. He hit him, first on one cheek and then on the other, and then again and again, until Mélanie thought he had gone mad. Toinon tried to pull his arm away, but her efforts were unsuccessful, and tears started to form at the corners of her eyes. Claude seemed to be choking over his sobs. Mélanie could hardly bear to look any longer, but, as suddenly as he had begun, Luc stopped. He knelt down on the ground and, circling Claude with both arms, he kissed his cheeks over and over. The whole incident left Mélanie dazed. If the guard had not moved just then to stand over them, she would have fallen into the nearest chair.

"Well," M. Guitard said, "that was quite a performance you got up for us!" Luc rose, and all four children stood in a rigid row, looking up at him. "Don't you know yet," the guard continued, "that you are forbidden to go on the grass? It seems to me that you have been coming to this park long enough to know these things. Well, now, let's see what the penalty is for such an offence . . ."

He took out a small black book and started leafing through it. Mélanie's knees were about to give way beneath her. She could not endure the thought of her brothers having to undergo any unknown suffering. "Whatever the punishment is," she thought, "I'll take it myself. After all, I'm the eldest," she reminded herself, "and if I ask politely but firmly, M. Guitard surely won't refuse."

Nurse had come up beside the guard. They exchanged a quick, conspiratorial glance.

"What are you going to do with them?" Nurse asked.

"Well," he said, with a chuckle, "since they are your charges, I think we'll have to let them off this time."

Nurse was about to protest, but M. Guitard closed his little black book, winked, and then asked if the embroidery she was working on was something she was making for him. Mélanie puzzled awhile over the wink. She could not make out whether it was intended for the children or if it was a special signal addressed to Nurse.

As the guard was about to start on his rounds again, he caught Mélanie's eyes watching him. "*Eh bien, mon enfant,*" he exclaimed, "what are you staring at?"

Mélanie did not answer. He took a few steps towards her, then, with his finger, beckoned her to come closer. She took her foot off the scooter and, pulling the two-wheeler with one hand, walked up to him.

"Mélanie," he chuckled, "don't look so serious." And as she remained silent, he added, "I'm sure your brothers won't do it again. I gave them a bit of a scare though, didn't I?" And he laughed, a gentle, self-satisfied laugh. "How old are you now?" he asked.

"Eight."

"Well, a girl of eight can still smile, no? Wait. I'll give you a nice puzzler to think about. Listen. How many people are you, do you suppose?"

And, clasping his hands behind his back, the guard waited for her answer. But Mélanie froze. Could it be that his policeman's eye had pierced right through her to her secrets? Speechless, she looked into his face.

"Listen. I'll tell you." Then, chuckling, he burst out, "Two! One and the same!"

But Mélanie whirled round, got on her scooter and raced away. She did not stop to see where her brothers might be now, but raced on, round a bend, down a winding path, across a wide alley, until she came to a halt by the park wall. Her mind was in a turmoil. She needed to be alone to still the whirling confusion of her thoughts. She was many people, of that she was certain. Many more than M. Guitard had any idea of. The number was staggering. Grown-ups, she well knew, were only two people; the one in front of children, and the one they changed into when a child had left the room or had gone to sleep.

Some of Mélanie's friends were many people; her brothers Claude and Luc and her sister Toinon were quite a few people, too. But she was the most. And this knowledge she kept to herself. She had many secrets stored in a hidden box somewhere within her chest. There were people she had been and things she had seen which she would have liked to talk over with her parents. But she could not. Such a dark cloud passed over their faces when she attempted to speak of something strange or terrible that she was forced to stop in the middle of a sentence. But more often it was the failure of her vocabulary which inhibited her. She could not find the words with which to describe the complexities of a feeling, and as she floundered, adults invariably became impatient and told her to run along, before she had finished.

Sometimes at night, before she fell asleep, the box would spring open, its contents would leap out, and, in all the confusion, she found herself face to face with questions she did not have the answer to; then she was afraid.

Her brother, Luc, sometimes had nightmares, and Mélanie knew that he, too, had a box, but she did not know what was in it. He shared his secrets only with Toinon who, though she was just five, always listened attentively to whatever Luc had to tell her. When his box got too full, she gently took the overflow and dropped it in her own.

Mélanie had no one to share her secrets with. She would have liked to talk to Claude, but he was too young to understand, too young to have a box of his own. Mélanie loved him so much that she did not want him to have one—ever.

The thought of Claude, his face perhaps still tear-stained, brought her abruptly back to the present. It must be almost tea-time, she thought. Slowly she scooted back towards Nurse.

She found her brothers and sister already biting into their bread and butter. There was no sign of the guard. One might have thought that nothing had happened. Mélanie pulled Luc aside.

"Why did you slap Claude like that?"

Luc looked at his sister but made no reply. Toinon sidled up beside him.

"Why?" Mélanie repeated.

Luc hesitated before answering. "I wanted him to cry, so I could kiss him afterwards."

"So he could console him," Toinon elucidated.

Mélanie stared at her brother and sister. Then, suddenly, she turned her head away and burst into tears.

LUC AND MÉLANIE WERE WALKING ON either side of their father on their way home from an exhibition. M. Abbot was explaining why it was that the paintings they had just seen were good but not first rate. Mélanie only dimly understood what he was saying; but it was a rare pleasure to have gone out with her father, and she felt very happy to be skipping beside him, in her best sky-blue coat and hat and her new white gloves.

If only she had not mistaken a Berthe Morisot for a Manet!

Her father had swooped down on her so suddenly. "Can't you see there is a difference in quality?" he had said, almost as if he were pleading with her.

She had nodded her head in assent, but she had not really seen the difference, and she was sorry to have caused that pained look in her father's eyes. She wondered if she would ever see, if she would ever know, all that her father knew. She gazed up at him. His head was turned away, looking into Luc's upturned face. They were talking about Seurat, and while Mélanie half-heard their words, she noticed anew how her father towered above the heads of passers-by. It was strange to think of his being a foreigner. She had difficulty sometimes remembering it. To his children he was "Papa," and it required an incongruous word or circumstance to shake them into a realization that he was not a Frenchman at all, but an American.

As they were about to cross the boulevard, M. Abbot let go of his children's hands, walked to the public urinal at the corner and disappeared behind its metal screen. His feet and the top of his hat were still visible; brother and sister kept their eyes on the latter in order not to lose him. But they need not have bothered. M. Abbot was still talking, "There's a Bonnard I want you to see at the Petit Palais . . ."

When he reappeared, they all three crossed the street. They were almost home when Mélanie saw an old woman leaning against a news-stand. The tips of her woollen gloves were cut off, and her exposed fingers held out a packet of shoe-laces. She looked very old and grey, and although her lips were moving and saying something, the pedestrians hurrying past seemed not to hear. She looked cold and she looked ill; and at the sight of her, a disturbing word sprang to Mélanie's mind. She had been told that across the unseen ocean, America was suffering from something called the Depression. She had heard the word many times and to her it had sounded like a disease, something like the Black Plague she had read about in her history book.

Her father was talking about Cézanne now, but Mélanie was no longer listening. She thought of her beloved grandfather and grandmother in the big house in Washington and wondered if they were in great pain. She had seen them the winter before when she and the whole family had crossed the Atlantic to visit them.

Tall, frail and thin, M. Abbot's parents had stood on their white porch to welcome the family. Mélanie had immediately loved her sweet and serene grandparents who had spoken such funny French and had seemed so glad to see them. She shuddered now, picturing them confined to their beds, still, and aflame with fever. She had often wanted to ask her father whether every American had a rash on his face or a temperature, but he frowned so when anyone mentioned the Depression that she dared not bring up the subject.

Here, in Paris, no one had the plague. Her best friend, Françoise, and all the people she knew were in good health. And yet, along the Rue de Rivoli one could see emaciated toy poodles displayed in gift shops and pastry shops. They were called *"chiens de crise."* Mélanie saw many children walking about the city with one of these "Depression dogs" clutched under their arms. But Mélanie did not want one. She thought of her grandparents all swollen with pimples and pain, and she did not want a dog.

LUC, TOINON AND MÉLANIE WERE SEATED at a small round table in the nursery. Nurse had placed three steaming bowls of soup in front of them before returning to the kitchen to have her own supper. Claude had already been fed and put to bed. Mélanie rose, walked over to her doll carriage and picked up Philippe le Bel, her doll. This doll was a handsome baby boy, almost two feet tall, whose curly hair, bland eyes and pouting mouth were all fashioned of wax. He had long ago lost his one-piece suit and now sat harmlessly in his emasculated altogether. For the past week, Mélanie had pulled up an extra chair to the table for Philippe le Bel and had fed milk and bread-crumbs into his hollow interior. His oval mouth was slightly opened, and tonight she was planning to share her soup with him. She, herself, did not like soup very much, but, having repeatedly been reminded of its nutritional value, she was deter-mined that her doll should have some. If this ritual inadvertently

lengthened the dinner hour, she saw no harm in it. She had just
seated the doll beside her, when Toinon with unaccustomed
firmness announced, "Tonight, Philippe le Bel will not eat with
us."

Mélanie looked at her sister, dumbfounded. Toinon, usually so
cheerful and obliging, now and then exhibited a surprising self-
assertiveness which never failed to baffle her.

"But he has to eat!" Mélanie stammered.

"He's not eating with us any more."

Under her mass of brown curls, Toinon's eyes were resolute.
Mélanie dipped her spoon in the home-made potato soup and
lifted it towards her doll's open mouth.

"*Non!*" Toinon cried. She tugged at the spoon until it overturned on the table-cloth.

"What's the matter?" Mélanie inquired angrily.

"Every day Luc and I have to wait for you to feed Philippe le
Bel, and then we have to wait until you've eaten. Well, we're
tired of waiting!"

"That's right," Luc broke in. "Toinon and I are always
through long before you, and Nurse won't bring the next course
until we've all finished."

"I don't care. My son has got to eat!"

Mélanie dipped her spoon once again into her steaming
bowl.

"I can't stand it any more . . ."

Toinon's voice trailed off. Her face was white. Her mouth was
set. Luc looked on placidly, as though he were the possessor of
infinite patience. As Mélanie picked up her spoon for the third
time, the silence was almost too loud to be borne. The spoon had
just found the doll's mouth, when Toinon screamed, "Enough!"
Seizing Philippe le Bel, she held him up in the air. The two girls
glared at each other, then Mélanie shouted, "Toinon!"

But Toinon whirled around and, clutching the doll to her

breast, fled from the room. Mélanie shot a glance at her brother. He sat, a serene, uncommitted Solomon. She dashed out in pursuit of her sister, who was running down the corridor. As Mélanie reached the library, she had a glimpse of her fleeing into the living-room. Toinon reappeared in the corridor, where she stopped a second, undecided. Seeing her sister behind her, she ran to the only remaining exit, the door leading to the kitchen stairs. Mid-way down the stairs, Mélanie almost caught up with her. The sisters tore through the pantry, past the startled servants seated at supper. Then, stopped by the stove, Toinon came to a halt in the kitchen. Before her, steam rose from a saucepan on the fire. She raised both arms and held the doll above it. Mélanie was now close enough to touch her sister's arm, but what she saw paralysed her, and, frozen to the spot, she stood watching helplessly. The doll's toes had begun to melt. Toinon, too, seemed transfixed. Like spun sugar, the doll's legs were thinning down and dripping slowly into the pan. When its waist narrowed into a thick, pink cascading dough, Mélanie, afraid she was going to be sick, clamped both hands on her stomach. Toinon suddenly let go of the doll, and as it fell with a splash into the pan, the overflowing liquid hissed over the surface of the stove.

"The soup!" It was the agonized cry of the cook. Madame Babette bent over her carefully spiced masterpiece. She turned round, her voice shaking. "How can I serve this mess to Monsieur and Madame!"

The two girls were leaning against opposite walls, pale and faint.

"You've ruined my soup!" The cook was close to tears.

"What's the meaning of this?" Nurse had finally recovered her speech.

"They're quite crazy," the maid said dispassionately.

But the accusing voices met with no response. Neither sister was listening.

"They had better go to bed," the maid added gently.

"Upstairs! Upstairs, you two!" Nurse urged them on.

In the nursery, Luc had finished his soup and was issuing orders to a platoon of tin soldiers, standing at attention on the table-cloth. His sisters did not even turn to look at the two plates of cold soup. Unprotesting, they allowed themselves to be put to bed. Before Nurse switched the light off, they looked at each other, but neither could find a word to say.

WITH LUC, MÉLANIE WAS OFTEN A VERY spiteful and, sometimes, an unhappy person. She enjoyed playing with her brother when he had his tin soldiers aligned on the floor. She would then pretend to be a boy, something big, like a colonel. She would fight hard, for she liked making a bloody mess of a battle until the fortress fell on its side and all the soldiers lay dead. Luc would then plead with her to stop, and accuse her of chipping off arms and legs and of ruining his toys. Or, if she raced her brother and won, Mélanie shouted loudly, wild with uncontrollable pride. Sister and brother fought, too, rolling on the floor and beating each other as hard as they could. Toinon, looking on, inevitably burst into sobs and, no matter who emerged the winner, ran to Luc, offering him one of her favourite toys to keep—for ever.

But playing at being a soldier had its perplexing aspects. Mélanie's mother would sometimes scold her for winning, since she was the eldest, and for having made Luc and Toinon burst into tears. Mélanie suspected her brother and sister of being tattle-tales, and she could not understand how her mother could believe all the things they had said, and the injustice of it made her want to cry until she felt all swollen inside.

At other times, she was a very grown-up person who went to the kitchen to ask for a biscuit, and then sat very erect and still on a stool and listened to the servants talk about their affairs. These were most complicated. They involved connivings, and whispers, conspiracies and shrieks of laughter. When Mélanie left the kitchen, she was sworn not to repeat a word. And, of course, she never did. The servants did many things and went to places that M. and Mme Abbot must not know about, and Mélanie understood that the servants' world was a different one from that of her parents or her own; and she could extend the image to the whole of Paris, where she sensed hundreds of worlds living side by side, each with a language and a code of its own, each forbidden territory to the other. And Mélanie felt like a very special person when she was allowed to sit in the kitchen.

One of her selves which she did not much like was the one who was Frank Fisher's girl. To be the girl of a boy who had not chosen you and whom you would never have picked for yourself, was disconcerting. The fact that Frank's father happened to be an American and M. Abbot's best friend made the situation all the more ticklish. It had all been M. Fisher's doing, for the pairing dated back to the picnic.

It had been a warm sunny day of early spring. M. and Mme Abbot and the Fishers, taking along several of their friends' children, had driven out to Chantilly and chosen a grassy clearing for their picnic site.

Mélanie, sitting cross-legged between Françoise de Béard and Frank Fisher, dunked her bread ceremoniously in a tin of watered wine. She ate in silence, only now and then grinning at her best friend who, lying on her stomach and eating a hardboiled egg, appeared to be enjoying herself immensely. Frank, as always, said little. Because of his incredible aptitude for passivity, Mélanie had difficulty remembering that he was not only present, but actually breathing and made of flesh and bone, like herself. If Amaury had not been sitting across from her, she might have thought of addressing a civil word or two to Frank, but as it was, she did not. She was really aware only of Françoise and Amaury. The latter was a friend the Abbot children had come to know on the beach in Kerouan, where they spent their summers. Mélanie had liked him from the start. He was a French boy, shorter than she, with curly brown hair and huge black eyes. She liked him not only because he wanted to grow up to be a concert pianist, but because he was soft-spoken and polite. It was fun being a boy with him. He never pulled her hair, or called her names or asked her to put up her fists, the way other boys did.

It was not long after the picnic baskets had been closed and the scattered debris put away, that Mélanie found herself caught within the dark tentacles of fate.

Amaury and she had picked up an old soggy rope they had found coiled on the ground, and were each idly tugging at one end of it when the other children saw them and came running to join in. Françoise, Toinon and the other girls rushed to Mélanie's side, while the boys, who were more numerous, lined up behind Amaury. The gentle pulling game that he and Mélanie had so innocently begun now turned into a most uneven tug-of-war. In spite of their valiant efforts, the girls found themselves being dragged off their feet. Mélanie was concentrating so hard on her hold of the rope that she was taken by surprise when her side gave an unexpectedly sharp tug and the boys lost their footing and pitched forward. She turned round. M. Fisher was standing right behind her. She looked into his pale, handsome face in astonishment. She heard herself shout, "No, no! Go away!"

Having an adult on the team was not fair play and, anyhow,

she did not want anybody feeling sorry for her because she was on the losing side. M. Fisher abruptly dropped the rope.

"Well, well, young lady, who do you take yourself for, a boy or something, playing such a game?"

He seemed amused, but Mélanie was not. She did not think it was any of his business to talk of one of her secret selves. She *was* a boy, and she was going to be one all day if she felt like it. In fact, she would remain one all day just to show him! M. Fisher moved over to where Frank was sprawled on the lawn, conversing with the grown-ups, and nudged him with his foot.

"Your girl-friend is having a tough time. Go give her a hand."

Mélanie was now close to tears with rage. It shocked her to hear M. Fisher use the word girl-friend. She was no one's girl-friend, and certainly not Frank's. She tugged at the rope more furiously than before. Frank got up, and she felt his weight on the rope behind her. He was tall for his ten years and strong, so that her team was able to offer the opposition some resistance, but the girls lost anyway. A jerk from the other side pulled Mélanie down on the grass, close to Amaury. He helped her up and, pointing to the far end of the clearing, he said, "Let's go and pick some flowers."

"I don't want to," Mélanie answered.

She ran off to pick up a ball and, aiming it at Frank, she called, "Throw it back to me!"

Amaury went off by himself, and Mélanie was a miserable boy all that day.

So it was, that, for reasons she did not totally comprehend, although she knew that in some subtle way it was due to that tug-of-war, her friends and her parents, too, came to consider Frank and herself as inseparable friends. At parties they were now seated next to each other and when children had to pair off in a game, she always found herself allied to Frank. She had, however, long ago come to the conclusion that certain things were permanent and immutable, the result of some mysterious but unbreakable law of the universe, like bedtime, and stewed peaches once a week, which she loathed, and stinging witch-hazel on cuts and sores, and now Frank as her special boy-friend.

Frank, too, seemed to have accepted his fate. If he brought to it no particular grace, neither did he show signs of rebellion. Perhaps this was because he was lazy or because, like Mélanie, he sensed the fatality of irrevocable laws. As a playmate she found him amiable but tiring. He had no ideas of his own, so that she was constantly in the position of having to think up things to do. He appeared to have a much better time when he was with Luc, but they never talked about this. Instead, they evolved a tacit understanding. When instinct told them that they had played together long enough to fulfil the obligations of their destined rôles, Frank moved away to play with Luc, while Mélanie went back to whatever she had been doing before the interruption.

IN THE LUXEMBOURG GARDENS IN THE afternoons, Mélanie became part of "the children." Together with her sister and brothers, she chose their friends and decided what games they would play. If Claude now and then wandered off to make mud-pies or explore life on his own, he was peremptorily recalled in times of crisis to stand by his elders.

The Luxembourg was divided into a variety of formal gardens, each a separate island with a character of its own and its particular habitués. Like migratory birds, each season, the same children returned daily to the section of the park they had made their own. An invisibly drawn line separated the children into three groups: those who came to the park with their mothers; those who came with their nurses or governesses; and the ones who came by themselves. The line dividing the first two groups was thin and could on occasion be crossed, but the boundary between the first two and the third was untraversable. This was part of the tribal law which, generation after generation, each child had to learn.

The Abbots belonged to the second group. This, to Mélanie, was predetermined and unchangeable, like so much of her life. And, perhaps, due to some innate fatalism in her temperament, she accepted it without questioning. Day in, day out, Nurse sat on the same chair amid congenial friends in a corner of the gardens which, though neither particularly spacious nor pretty, did contain something unique. This was a long, narrow, gently sloping strip of tarred road, intended for the use of bicycles, roller skates and tricycles.

For a very long time, Mélanie, her sister, and Luc merely stood on the edge of the tarred road, watching the children who played there, but never trespassing. "The road," as it was called, was in the possession of children who came to the park with their mothers. The Abbots and their playmates had to content themselves with wheeling their scooters on the stone-strewn dirt paths. The laws were ancient and larger than life, but perhaps envy was outside the law.

As the months rolled by, Mélanie became quite familiar with the faces that zoomed past her on the road; she even learned the names of some of them. And one day, it happened. With Luc and Toinon, she stood as usual, waiting in silence for someone to go by, but no one did. The other children were gathered at the head of the decline and appeared to be engrossed in serious conversation. There seemed to be some disagreement, too, for voices were raised. Disappointed, the Abbots started to move away when someone called, "*Et*, Luc, Mélanie! Wait a minute!"

A boy, a little older than Mélanie, waved from the centre of the agitated group and signalled them to wait. The onlookers stood transfixed and mute. They had been addressed. Surely something of great moment was about to take place. A few seconds went by, then the group moved towards them with the older boy in the lead.

"We've decided," he said, "to let you three use the road."

Mélanie felt a bright coloured arrow shoot from out her heart, past her head and up into the sky. Luc opened his mouth wide, but could say nothing, and Toinon's large brown velvety eyes were now enormous. There was a brief pause caused by pent-up joy and stunned disbelief. Then Mélanie spoke. She said what she knew had to be said, "*Merci*. But we can't unless you allow our friends to use it, too."

She was answered by disgusted moans and groans. The leader, whose name was René, asked, "How many are you?"

"Eight, all together."

The little group moved a few feet away to reform a circle. A new discussion was on. Finally, René came back to say, "For the moment, it's just you three. We'll see about the rest."

Mélanie, Luc and Toinon thanked them and rushed for their scooters. They raced up and down the road twenty times. This was a day they would remember for ever.

When the headiness of the first few days had ebbed away, the chosen ones started to feel uneasy. Their position as guests of the competing group had unwittingly made them traitors to their own. Seeing their old playmates standing by the edge of the road, as once they had stood, made them feel both disloyal and set apart. They ceased playing on the road.

Some weeks later, René asked Mélanie the reason for her desertion. She explained how this special dispensation had thrown

a bridge between herself and her former friends. René nodded his head and announced, "I'll call another meeting."

The following day he asked the Abbots and their friends to meet him at the head of the road. He told them that his group had agreed to let the newcomers use the road on condition that they follow the rules to the letter. If anyone of them broke a rule, all eight would be ousted. Mélanie assented. René proceeded to list the rules.

The first, naturally enough, was concerned with keeping out group number three—those who came to the park alone. Should they threaten to take the road by force, everyone was bound to fight to the finish. René was the leader. His title was President. All disputes must be brought to his attention, and parents and nurses were not to be called in as arbiters. No change of policy could be made without a meeting of all members. A boy, André, directed traffic at the intersection where the road crossed a wide alley. He carried a whistle, and his signals must be obeyed. Snitching another's property was strictly forbidden. A girl provided with Elastoplast and iodine was the nurse, and bench number four was the first-aid station. René or the traffic policeman had the final say as to who was at fault when two vehicles collided. Bad language, the use of horns and insults learned from cab drivers were not only permitted but even *de rigueur*.

The reasonableness of the rules made them easily acceptable. The agreement was sealed with handshakes and introductions.

For the newcomers this was the beginning of a new and marvellous era. And when Mélanie scooted down the road, she imagined herself the fastest and most daring woman on wheels, who would one day own a bicycle and win the *Tour de France*. She pictured fires, cave-ins, floods; and she, Mélanie, racing alone, fearless, to attend to the rescue single-handed, shortly to be decorated with the *Légion d'honneur* and admired the rest of her life. So, on the road, she was a hero.

and one of them was the woman in love. She was in love, not with a boy but with a man—a man who, unlike those in fairy tales, did not return her love. This only mildly disturbed her, for she attributed his blindness to the slowness inherent in all adults to see and grasp the emotional crux in the simplest of situations. She was certain that given time, he would come to his senses.

He was in his early twenties. Sometime before, he had left his home in Bayonne and bidden farewell to his bewildered and disappointed parents, in order to study music in the capital. While preparing for a career as a concert pianist, he lived in a boarding house near the Abbots. Since musical instruments were not available there, a friend had persuaded Mme Abbot to allow him the use of her grand piano.

Mélanie could still remember that day two years ago when he had walked into the living-room for the first time. Mme Abbot had called in Luc and Mélanie and their tutor, Mlle Denis, to introduce them and to explain that the young man would be practising in the mornings while they were having their lesson. She hoped it would not prove too distracting to their studies. Mlle Denis had blushed and protested that it would not disturb anything at all, and Luc had jumped up and down and tugged at his mother's sleeve, to ask if the young man might teach him to play, too. But Mélanie had neither moved nor said a word. She could only gaze mutely at the stranger, who stood politely erect and silent while Mme Abbot explained the routine of the household.

Tall and blond, he had eyes set in a deep cavern below bushy eyebrows and a high forehead. His eyelids were heavy and opened so slowly that the clear blue of his eyes came as a shock. His fingers were long and thin, like his legs, and Mélanie had had to look up almost to the ceiling to see him whole. His unsmiling

26

face had a grave, melancholy air, which brought to her mind all the disguised princes who had ever wandered about their narrow kingdoms in search of their true destiny.

Had the young man been carried in on a sedan chair, all dressed in silks and laces, instead of the blue serge suit he actually wore, he could not have seemed to her more beautiful or more like every Cinderella's ideal of the unknown prince.

When Mélanie found herself being gently propelled out of the room by Mlle Denis, she felt as if her heart had suddenly been transformed into a glowing ember, which not only warmed her whole being but could pierce the impenetrable shadows of the world about her.

SHORTLY BEFORE CHRISTMAS, MME ABBOT asked her daughter what she wanted from *le père Noël*. Mélanie knew exactly what she wanted.

"A baby sister," she said.

Claude was over three years old and hardly a baby any more. She wanted a real baby to hold and cuddle. When her mother said, "But *le père Noël* only brings toys," Mélanie was undeterred.

"He'll know where to find me a baby sister."

She believed in *le père Noël* and his ability to read her mind. So, happily, she waited for Christmas and a new sister.

When Mélanie had asked where babies came from, she had received a diversity of answers. Some babies were found in cabbages, for instance; some were on sale on the top floor of the Bon Marché; some women carried their babies inside them, under their bulging coats; and, in Alsace, children were dropped on church spires by flying storks. She did not much care where *le père Noël* found his babies. She was certain that he knew just where to look and would find the right one.

Le père Noël came to Europe on Christmas Eve; this gave him time to reach America on Christmas Day, when he would take her cousins in Washington their presents. On the twenty-third of December, the fireplace was scrubbed and swept clean of ashes. The most comfortable chair was placed in front of it and a small table pulled up next to the chair. A steaming cup of coffee, one cigarette and a box of matches were arranged neatly on the table. This gave *le père Noël* a chance to rest before continuing his journey. One cigarette was surely all he had time for on such a busy night! And since he always gave presents without ever asking for any himself, the Abbot children left him a memento of their own making, usually a drawing, a poem or a piece of embroidery.

Bedtime was early that evening. Children kept their eyes tight shut and tried hard to go to sleep. Occasionally a voice would startle the darkness.

"Toinon, are you asleep?"

"Almost."

"Hurry up!"

And later: "Are you still awake, Luc?"

"Yes, but I'm trying."

And morning was suddenly here! There was a mad dash to the fireplace before breakfast. The coffee had been downed to the last dreg. A cigarette butt lay crumpled in the saucer. The small gifts were gone. The fireplace was streaked with soot. He had come!

This was the longest day Mélanie ever had to live through. She was conscious of the pounding of her own heart, and food would not go down. Grande-Tante came after lunch and took the young Abbots for a walk in the park. Children formed themselves into groups, exchanging hopes and expectations. Now and then, some older child attempted to throw a doubt as to *le père Noël's* existence; but his cynicism was quickly rejected as an exhibition of unwarranted arrogance. Then, at last, the return home, and baths and clean clothes and suppertime.

M. and Mme Abbot and Grande-Tante were already in the living-room to light the tree. Supper remained unfinished, as four children stood expectant at the door. Suddenly it was thrown open and three grown-up voices sang out, "*Joyeux Noël!* Merry Christmas!"

The tree, ablaze with candles, glimmered tall and magical, while a riot of colour, ribbons and packages circled its base. Prominently displayed were roller skates for Luc, a car big enough for Claude to sit in, and a doll's house for Toinon. Mélanie's eyes made a quick survey. There, on a chair, sat her baby sister all dressed in white. She rushed towards her, then stopped short. Something was wrong! The baby neither wriggled her toes nor made a gurgling sound but gazed, unblinking, into space. She hardly seemed to be breathing. Mélanie bent down and lightly touched her arm. She was dead. No, it was a doll! Disappointment, like a fluid, ran from her heart down to her toes. She could not think of a thing to say. She looked and looked at the doll. Had she made a mistake, would she still, perhaps, come alive? The doll stared back at her from her deep still eyes. Mélanie gradually became aware of a vast silence in the room, but she did not dare turn round and face the mute stare of her family. She waited a second more before picking up the doll, and, studying her, she noticed that she was the size Philippe le Bel had been, only her eyes were a clear blue, her hair, soft and black.

"Her name is Nadine," Mélanie announced whirling round. She walked over to the couch, sat down and rocked her doll to sleep.

for tea in celebration of Epiphany. As was customary on Twelfth Night, Mme Babette, the cook, had baked a fluffy, multi-layered cake without icing, and into the dough she had slipped a ring, a thimble and other treasures; the most important being a tiny porcelain doll, representing the child Jesus, in swaddling clothes. Whoever found the doll in his, or her, slice of cake was king or queen for the day and could, in turn, crown a mate, for tradition demanded that there be two paper crowns on the table.

Amaury and, of course, Frank Fisher were among the guests. The children played hide-and-seek before tea, and Mélanie had shown Amaury her favourite hiding place behind a curtain in the library. As they huddled together, intensely awaiting discovery, he whispered to her, "If I happen to be crowned, will you be my queen?"

"Yes, and if I find the infant Jesus, I'll make you king."

And to secure the pact, they shook hands on it.

When the time came for tea, the children were called into the dining-room. Mélanie looked at the table and wondered if she had ever seen it so prettily laid. There were favours at every child's place and coloured napkins, and in the centre, almost too dazzling to believe, were the two crowns—a gold one for the king, a silver one for the queen.

Mélanie sat down at the head of the table, and Frank sat opposite her, his back to the living-room door, where his parents stood watching with M. and Mme Abbot. Mélanie asked her father to cut the cake. The children watched soberly to see that he cut the slices evenly. There was a slight pause, as M. Abbot admired his handiwork; then plates were passed round. Mélanie's turn was last, and she had difficulty repressing her excitement. She exchanged a knowing glance with Amaury, then allowed her empty plate to be passed up to her father. No one spoke, as each child poked tentatively into his share of cake. Even the grown-ups looking on were silent. With her fork, Mélanie carefully cut out a bite-size piece before gingerly inserting it into her mouth.

Luc let out a happy squeal when a gold goblet fell on his plate, and Toinon's young friend, Geneviève, beamed contentment as she extracted the ring from her mouth. Mélanie cut into her cake once more, and there was the baby! She said, "Oh!," and held it up for all to see. She smiled at the grown-ups standing in the doorway and met her mother's eyes. Mme Abbot appeared agitated. She was pointing at something or someone. Mélanie then looked at her father. He, too, was making odd jerky motions. Both of them were pointing to Frank's back. Her glance passed to the Fishers; they were watching her with smug parental assurance. Oh no! she thought. She closed her hand on the porcelain doll and remained motionless, her arm in the air. She looked at Amaury. He was grinning at her, but she could not answer his smile. Her eyes turned back to question her parents once more; their gestures were growing wilder. Something like a stone rose in Mélanie's throat, then came down again and fell into the box inside her. She picked up the gold crown and handed it to Frank.

"Thanks," he said, "Now put yours on."

But she did not move. Frank left his seat and walked around the table to place the crown upon her head. The maid was passing the ice-cream; everyone was talking again. The grown-ups returned to the living-room. Mélanie could not look at Amaury.

After tea, they played pin-the-tail-on-the-donkey, and still she could not look at Amaury. She wanted to wait until they were alone to explain, but the opportunity did not present itself. When the young guests finally took their leave, he came up to thank her parents. After he had said what a nice time he had had, Mélanie stretched out her hand and stammered, "Amaury . . ."

And he said, "Yes, Mélanie . . ." and children and parents crowded the door, and before she could assemble her words, Amaury had been pushed outside on the landing.

It would be many weeks before she could face him again, and the stone lay heavy in her box with all the other secrets.

IT IS NOT A SIMPLE THING, MÉLANIE thought, to be a girl and to be good. She did not know why she had taken all the furniture out of Toinon's doll's house and shunted the miniature carpets and pictures all around until they were in the wrong place.

When Toinon had tried to stop her, pulling at her arms and shouting, "No, no, Mélanie! No!" she knew she had been bad and had wanted to be bad. Now she was sitting on the small chair in the nursery, watching her sister putting her house back in order, and she wondered why she had been bad and why it was she was not through being bad. For she was not through. She thought and thought, then rose and went down to the kitchen. She was glad to find the cook alone.

"Hello, Mme Babette," she said as sweetly as she could. "Maman would like to speak to you."

When, after washing her hands, the cook had gone in search of Mme Abbot, Mélanie climbed on a chair, reached for the sugar box on the top shelf and took out five cubes. She hurried back to the nursery. She had barely settled herself in her chair when Mme Babette came in to ask what kind of mischief she was up to! Mélanie opened her eyes as far as she could, in an effort to look both surprised and grand.

33

The cook muttered angrily, "It's one of your tricks again," then slammed the door and shuffled down the hall.

Mélanie could see herself getting worse and worse. She took the five pieces of sugar from her smock pocket, lined them up neatly on her knees and then started to suck one.

"Where did you get those?" Luc asked from his sitting position on the floor, where he was pushing a toy truck.

"Nowhere."

"Did Mme Babette give them to you?"

"No."

Mélanie felt delightfully sphinx-like.

"How did you get them then?" Luc persisted.

"None of your business," she replied.

"A little piece for Claude?"

Claude nuzzled against her. He could be so disgustingly greedy.

"No," she said, but she would not turn and look at his face.

"She's selfish," Toinon interjected, still busy with her house.

"That's right," Mélanie agreed, glad to have her sister know her for what she really was.

Luc stood up.

"If you don't give us each a piece, I'll tell on you," he threatened.

"I won't!" And she put another cube in her mouth.

"Share!" Luc ordered, "or you'll get spanked."

Mélanie quickly shoved another piece in her mouth. This one tasted the worst of the three. Luc opened the door to the corridor.

"Don't!" Toinon pleaded, her loyalties torn.

Luc looked at her and replied with false bravado. "We must!"

As the door closed behind him, the two sisters exchanged an uneasy glance. Claude nervously broke the silence.

"Ooh . . . spanking!" and hastened to busy himself in a corner of the room.

Mélanie bit into another cube. This time she was going to be sick. She threw the last piece into the doll carriage. The room was oppressively silent. She was debating with herself whether to hum or not, when Luc returned, quiet and enigmatic. Her three judges were pretending, each in his corner, to be intensely busy. The silence persisted. It was broken by Nurse's entrance.

"Mélanie, is it true that you've stolen some sugar?"

No one made a sound.

"Mélanie, answer me!"

"I took it for my doll," Mélanie said, after an uncomfortable silence.

She felt tired now. She could think of nothing to say, so she added feebly, "She's hungry."

"You are not to go to the kitchen to take sugar or anything else, do you hear? Bring me the sugar."

Mélanie pointed to the doll carriage. "It's in there."

"Bring it to me!"

Nurse certainly was a tyrant and a pain. Mélanie got up, rescued the one remaining cube and handed it to Nurse.

"Bring me the rest."

"That's all."

Mélanie felt utterly weary. She could feel her brothers' and sister's eyes on her, but she knew they were pretending very hard not to be there.

"Bring me the rest," Nurse repeated.

"I ate them," Mélanie finally admitted.

And all at once she felt a strong hand slap her firm behind. Her body tingled from head to foot. She felt herself being dragged into the bedroom and put down on her bed. The light went out, and she was alone. She did not feel bad any more. She was just sore all over. She turned and tossed in the dark and wondered why it was that little girls sometimes wanted to be good and couldn't.

pianist resumed his daily practising at the keyboard, Mélanie crept into the living-room with her doll and went to sit beneath the piano. She swayed under the gathering momentum of the pedals and allowed her ears to be so filled with the vibrating sounds that the music seemed to be emanating from somewhere within her, rather than invading her. She liked to sit here, imagining herself floating on the chords, as if on a wave. When the sound died away, she felt as though the sea had swallowed her into its depthless silence. Then as the melody began again, she was lifted back to the liquid centre of sound. Today she could share these sensations with Nadine. As she peered into her doll's eyes, she noticed for the first time that they were the same colour blue as those of the young man at the piano. Now, perhaps, Nadine could claim a father.

Mélanie rose from her hiding place and went to stand by the young man. He looked up.

"Nicholas," she said, "this is my baby. *Le père Noël* brought her."

"She's lovely," he said, casting a quick sidelong glance at the doll, which she held extended before him. "Pretty blue eyes."

Mélanie was about to point out their striking resemblance to his own, but his arms were already raised, ready to strike a chord. He was playing once more. She returned to her place under the piano and hugged her doll and told her not to cry.

Later, wheeling her doll carriage in the park, Mélanie decided to keep the identity of Nadine's father to herself, believing it wiser to withhold this information from casual acquaintances. Other dolls had fathers, but seldom a real one, for the majority of young mothers preferred imaginary swains, who could be replaced at will when the old ones had lost their freshness. But she would have liked to share her secret with Françoise and wished that her friend played in the Luxembourg Gardens, instead of in the Parc Monçeau. For although Françoise was very grown-up and serious and had little use for dolls, she had always shown an aunt-like interest in Philippe le Bel. She was bound to care as much, if not more, for Nadine when she met her. But without her friend to talk to, Mélanie sometimes joined other mothers of dolls to discuss clothes, babies' eating habits and the weighty responsibility of motherhood. Sitting all in a row, the girls pushed their carriages forward and backward until they had rocked their dolls to sleep. They brought bits of material to sew on, or pieces of embroidery pulled taut across a wooden ring. But Mélanie had no sewing. She worked instead on her imaginary knitting. Clutching an invisible ball of wool under her left armpit, she wove her fingers in and out, and when she lost a stitch, she let out a small wail of pain, as she had heard her mother do.

But one day André called to her, while she was busy knitting, and asked her to come to a meeting of the road. René had moved away some weeks before, whether to another city or merely to a different section of the park had not been clearly ascertained. In any case, André was calling a special meeting for the election of new officers. All the children gathered in a clumsy circle, and it soon became obvious that no one had given the matter any previous thought. There was an awkward silence. André said, "Well," but he appeared ill at ease and unsure as to how to proceed.

He was a fat, kindly boy, but no leader. Everyone's eyes wandered about the group in search of a strong character, a winning, dominant personality who could be entrusted with authority, but no one stood out. André, too, was vainly sizing up with his eyes. He turned abruptly, as though struck by a thought, to the boy beside him and asked, "What does your father do?"

"Grocer," the boy replied.

"And yours?" he asked the next boy.

"Civil servant."

André had hit upon a means of elimination which was hierarchically acceptable, for like father, like son. The tight circle loosened and relaxed. Questions and answers were coming quickly. Mélanie felt fear sweep over her. In a few minutes, no . . . seconds, she, too, would have to answer the question, and she did not know. She had no idea what her father did, except that every day he went to what he called the office—a handsome suite of rooms, lined with books and etchings. Children waiting for their father could look out of the french windows at the Seine and the bright sweep of Paris roofs, but they had to be very quiet and must not be heard to speak above a whisper, as Mlle Pêcher took M. Abbot's dictation in French or Miss Blair took it in English.

Mélanie looked at Luc and then at Toinon. They were looking at her, a questioning look on their faces. She could see that no help would come from them. She thought and thought, but no clue came to her. Then she remembered something. Her father had once dropped a visiting card from his wallet, and Mélanie had had a chance to glance at it as she picked it up for him. His name was printed in the centre of it in dark letters and, on the lower right-hand side in smaller print was written: *President*. Mélanie had not been able to decipher the rest. President? But president of what, she simply did not know. And now André was asking her the question. Her voice was firm as she answered, but her body was shaking. "Papa is president," she said.

There was a pause. The fearful second question did not come. Instead André asked, "Where does he work?"

"At the office," Mélanie replied. Her confidence was returning. This she knew.

"Where is his office?" André continued.

"That way," and Mélanie pointed towards the sky, over the trees and beyond the park. Every child turned to follow the direction of her upraised arm. Between the trees and the roof of the Senate, the old Medici Palace, glimmered in the sun. André came closer and asked, "He's president of what?"

There it was, at last, the question she had fearfully waited for; but she was not given time to search her beclouded memory once again, for a boy, speaking with great assurance, answered for her, "He must be President of the Republic, you idiot!"

And Mélanie all at once knew this to be the correct answer. That her father was an American and occasionally put an alien emphasis on a French syllable, only stirred the faintest ripple of doubt on the loyal waters of her mind. Since France had to have a president for its Republic, it was only natural, not to say blatantly obvious, that the only man fit for such a job was her father. A handsomer, wiser, more dignified man France had not seen since Charlemagne. It was a relief to know why he hurried off to the office every day.

The circle had shifted, and the Abbots found themselves standing in the centre of it. A silent, serious ring of children moved slowly around them, studying them with the care of a farmer buying a pig at market. Mélanie looked down at herself, then her glance passed over Luc, Toinon and Claude. All four were dressed in identical light coats, with white shoes and socks. For the first time, she became aware of the fact that they were the only ones in white shoes and socks.

"*Président de la République, peut-être . . .*" André said, more to himself than to anyone in particular.

Mélanie stood dazed, conscious for the first time in her life, of a difference between herself and her playmates. Lost, she stood in contemplation of the thought. When André tapped her on the shoulder, he seemed to have come from very far away.

"You're President of the Road, then," he said and shrugged his shoulders.

He turned to Luc. "You're in charge of traffic."

André appointed Toinon the new nurse. She smiled her acceptance happily, but when he explained that she had to care for the wounded, she burst out with an agonized, "No, no, no!"

"She's awfully young," André muttered reflectively, "but..." and he shrugged his shoulders again.

The elections were over. There had been no dissenting vote.

IT WAS IN THE SUMMER THAT MÉLANIE WAS happiest, for summer meant Kerouan in Brittany, and she loved the smell of rocks and the sight and sound of the sea. Morning and afternoon, children were free to roam the beach, digging their bare toes into the warmth of its yellow sand, or to walk over rocks to lift mussels and tease sea anemones, astir in small isolated pools. And the stone had a perfume when it was dry and another when the sea had just washed over it, and to Mélanie this was the smell of life. With miniature nets on wooden poles, she and her friends fished for shrimps along the shore, and to show how brave they were, they sometimes ate a live one. Mélanie tried to imagine how the shrimp felt, then she would try not to think of it at all.

She swam in shallow water and was sometimes cold and often scared by the deceiving stillness of this sea which could engulf her, leaving no trace, no echoing sound. But she never wanted to come out. She could watch the ocean for ever, and she fancied that by looking at the sky in the mornings, she could anticipate the kind of day that lay ahead, whether the sea would have white caps back almost to the horizon, or whether it would stretch a deep still blue or rage a turbulent green. She kept track of the tides in order to visualize which rocks might still be wet and which ones quite dry. She watched the Atlantic and wondered how she could ever live away from it, and yet the sea frightened her, and at times she could not bear looking at it any longer. The ocean was so vast, so still and yet so clamorous, so changeable and yet immovable, that it left her speechless with questioning. She mused over the fishes, and the seaweed and the mystery in the deep centre of the ocean, over which she had sailed only the year before for America. She wondered if the sea were God— and the blurred image of her Maker was always slightly watery.

The French sky in summer was often a deep blue, sprinkled with white clouds, lighter than spun sugar and swollen like puffs of cotton. These moved merrily and silently above Mélanie's head and, though she liked to watch them go by, she did not feel towards the sky as she did towards the sea. No gods hid there to disturb her, even though she had heard that the Virgin Mary moved somewhere up there to intervene for the dying. The sky seemed far away, remote and gay; the sea was here at her feet, moody, rumbling and deep.

In the mornings, M. Lachaise held gymnastic classes on the beach at Kerouan. The classes were divided according to age groups. Children under five came first, and the responsibility of seeing that Claude got to his class on time had fallen on Mélanie. Most of the time Claude offered no resistance, and, taking hold of his sister's hand, trotted nicely beside her. But there were times when he did not want to go. He would sit tightly on the sand and scream. "Nurse! Luc! Toinon!" until they all promised to come along. Or he would not budge. If they refused to come, he would rise suddenly and start to run until Mélanie caught him and forcefully dragged him to class, while he cried, or pretended to. Mélanie loved to stay and watch this class, it was so enchantingly chaotic.

M. Lachaise would line up the little ones, then blow his whistle, bend from the waist, and as he touched his feet with his hands, he would shout "One, two! One, two!" Some children stood and watched him, as though he were doing these strange things to entertain them; others would bend over and fall on their sides, while some simply wandered off and away. Mme Lachaise, who was always at hand to help and advise, would run in pursuit of the deserters and then rush back to seize a child about to fall off the climbing frame.

So many individual phobias were expressed in this class that M. Lachaise was eventually forced to give up all his whistling, and to leave each of his charges to his particular compulsion. There were balls to play with and ropes to jump; and Mélanie like to help the Lachaises keep a semblance of order, as the hour was punctuated by bursts of sudden giggles or inexplicable tears. Claude would roll over in the sand like a puppy freed of his leash, or climb a few rungs of the ladder, bellowing delightedly, *"Regardes, Méli! Regardes-moi!"*

And his sister would look, for he was the most wonderful child of all.

The next class was attended by the three older Abbots. It consisted of twenty to thirty pupils who lined up according to size and did exercises in unison. Mélanie enjoyed this class, but in a fearful way.

M. Lachaise was intense, incredibly tanned and nimble. Year in and year out, he wore a navy blue beret, a pair of brown, immaculately pressed trousers, and a shiny white under-vest. About his neck a whistle dangled from a cord; but most of the time it was in his mouth. He blew it constantly, it seemed, from eight in the morning until noon. When he was not blowing it, he was shouting in a hoarse, terrifying voice, all the while drooling at both corners of his mouth. Now and then he sent a long, high-flying spit into the sand. When his pupils had taken their position in four neat rows, he would read out the roll call, bellowing each child's complete name. Mélanie would stand, straight and alert, in order to answer "Present!" as soon as he had read out, loud enough for the whole beach and all the ships at sea to hear: "Mélanie Marie Abbot." If some child did not respond immediately, he would look up from his sheets with a look of bewilderment and stammer hoarsely, "But where is he?"

And if the child was absent and could not reply, M. Lachaise would turn to look at his wife with the agonized stare of a man who felt the earth giving way under his feet. Mme Lachaise, who never ventured more than a few feet away, would nod reassuringly. His cheek muscles would loosen, a sly foolish smile would pass over his face, only to vanish as quickly as it had come. And if there was a second silence in the roll call, he would start the whole performance over again.

Mélanie was a good pupil and was often chosen to show the others how a certain exercise ought to be done. But when the young gymnasts were made to stand up straight to show off their posture, a dreadful thing always happened. M. Lachaise's eyes would move down the row and, as they came to rest on her, a look of horror would come into them, and he would scream, "Mélanie, feet together!" as though the last breath had gone out of him.

She would then send a look of supplication towards Mme Lachaise, who would say slowly and calmly, "Jean, you know she can't."

The instructor stared a second at Mélanie before letting out an earth-shattering sigh. If she put her feet together, her knees would be in front of one another; if she placed her knees together, her feet stood wide apart. She herself could not understand why this was. She alternated the position every other day in the hope, devoid of faith, that one day both she and the instructor would find her legs straight and parallel all the way down. If it had not been for Mme Lachaise's quiet acceptance of her physical peculiarity, Mélanie could not have endured the torture of this daily exposure.

Mme Lachaise was tall and statuesque, with her husband's tanned skin. She had huge, sad, beautiful eyes, and she was the most gentle and patient woman Mélanie had ever known. Once in a while, she would put her arms around the girl and hug her, and Mélanie loved her immeasurably. Since M. Lachaise never spoke, but kept his voice at a shouting pitch, he occasionally screamed at his wife, too; this made Mélanie wince. But Mme Lachaise always answered him softly, smiling as though he had just whispered some endearment. Mélanie had mixed feelings towards M. Lachaise. She felt there was something ominous in his constant drooling and his sudden wild alarms.

She once timidly asked Mme Lachaise why her husband screamed at her every day about her feet not being together. Mme Lachaise replied, "He's a good man, but he forgets." Since Mme Lachaise would certainly never tell a lie, Mélanie had to believe that he was a good man, but she feared him almost as much as if he had been a bad one.

ONE SULTRY AUGUST MORNING MÉLANIE was sitting on the stone steps of her family's house in Kerouan, called *Le Roc*, watching Jean-Baptiste burning the rubbish. Although the old gardener had lost all of his teeth, he still retained a healthy crown of red hair, on top of which perennially perched a weather-beaten brown cap. Whenever he was asked a question which required some deliberation, he pushed his cap to the back of his head with thumb and forefinger, in order to scratch his forehead with his little finger. He chewed tobacco between his gums and before making a reply of any kind, he spat out a generous wad over his left shoulder. His profane vocabulary was rich and wide, but he used it sparingly and with the deepest of feeling, for he was a man of few words. Kind, hard-working and earnest, he was stubbornly loyal to the family and devoted to the children. He never minded being interrupted for hugs or kisses or questions. The odour of tobacco rose from him at all times; and though Mélanie had never been quite sure whether or not she liked the smell, she did know that if he smelled any differently, he would not be Jean-Baptiste, but another man altogether.

From the stone steps she could see his every movement. She liked to watch the ease with which he lifted the pitchfork to plunge it into the fire. As the wind changed, he moved a step or two around the wire basket. There was a quiet rhythm to everything he did, which made her think of him as something timeless and rooted, like a bush or a tree.

From the wire basket a tall flame rose; it was so high and startling that, without knowing what she was about to do or say, Mélanie leapt up from the steps and ran to Jean-Baptiste. She encircled his waist with her arms, dug her nails into his belt and heard herself cry out: "Where is Lucie? Where is Lucie?"

A terrible sickness came into her stomach, so that she could not think but could only hold on to the gardener's waist with all the strength of her arms. She hardly understood her own words. Lucie had been gone over three years, but her name had sprung unbidden from Mélanie's lips, and a wordless distress shook her whole body.

The gardener carefully put down the pitchfork, then, pushing back his cap, he scratched his forehead and spat. A gentle hand came down to rest on her head, and finally he spoke. "There, there, *ma jolie*. Who knows where she is? Far from here, that's for sure. There, there."

One hand cradling her head, he rocked her gently against his bony chest. Mélanie was not crying, for it was something young ladies did not do; only peasant children cried. But a great swelling had distended the walls of her head, so that it felt heavy and about to burst. Suddenly she could not endure the sight of the flaming rubbish any longer; she pulled herself free from the consoling arms and dashed into the house. She barely heard Jean-Baptiste calling to her: "Forget her, little one! Forget her!"

In the living-room Mme Abbot was talking to a friend. Mélanie backed away. In the pantry, Nurse was ironing. No interruption would be welcomed there. Upstairs in the nursery, Toinon and Luc were playing with a pack of cards. In his room, Claude sat on the floor making a tower of blocks and talking to himself. Mélanie walked in.

"Claude," she said, and he looked up. "Lucie is gone for good."

But her little brother made no reply. He only stared at her as though she were going to say more, as though she had begun a story. It was long ago, when Mélanie was five, that Lucie had left, and of course, Claude had not been born yet. He could not possibly understand. No one, not even Claude, to talk to. Mélanie threw herself on the narrow bed and wept like a peasant.

Lucie was in the box in Mélanie's chest. Why the lid should have opened at that moment, she did not know. Lucie had been Mme Abbot's maid but when Mélanie was born, Lucie loved her so much that she spent all her spare time in caring for her. She did this so well that, if the cleaning got a bit careless and superficial, it was overlooked. When Luc came along a year later, a cleaning woman was brought in once a week, and the maid continued her ministrations. But when, two years later, there was a third baby, Mme Abbot engaged Nurse to take over. Lucie was once again consigned to the housework. Only on the nurse's day off was she allowed to take charge of the children. It had been Mélanie's favourite day of the week. But she often managed to follow Lucie around as she carried her cleaning equipment from room to room, and then she could tell the maid how much she loved her. There were, however, tensions and jealousy between nurse and maid that Mélanie did not know of. If the Abbot children had once or twice caught Lucie in tears, or heard Nurse slam the kitchen door, these were but the auguries, which children may not question but must endure, of that awesome other world in which adults move and from which they rule.

The family was at *Le Roc* that fateful summer of Mélanie's fifth birthday. On a day in late July, she had felt that she was a new and very strange person. She had been moody, restless and teary and had refused to finish her supper. She had not known why she was this person, but a few days later she became aware of a dreadful thing. She had not seen Lucie for two days.

"Where is Lucie?" she had asked Nurse, but the nurse had turned away and would not answer.

"Where is Lucie?" she asked her mother.

"Lucie has gone back to Paris, but Brigitte is coming tomorrow, and you'll love Brigitte . . ."

Her mother, she could see, was prepared to go on, but Mélanie fled. She had not wanted to hear any more. She ran to the kitchen.

"Mme Babette," she asked, "why has Lucie gone away?"

"It's that nurse," the cook answered, an ugly inflection to her voice. "She wouldn't let Lucie near you children, and you know how terribly fond of you all Lucie is."

"Yes, but I love her!" Mélanie wailed.

"Now, now," Mme Babette gurgled as she lifted Mélanie on

47

to her lap. And the rocking chair swung back and forth, as the cook held tightly to the weeping child.

It had been a long and lonely day for Mélanie. In the afternoon, she had kicked shells with her toes along the wet sand. She had not wanted to play with anyone.

At supper time, Luc seemed unusually silent. Mélanie had not had a word to say to him. When her parents came into the dining-room to bid them goodnight before going out, Mélanie had risen and thrown her arms around her mother. "Maman! Maman!" she shouted.

She could find no other words with which to frame her question or express her distress. Mme Abbot held her awhile and patted her absently, but then she left the room.

At *La Roc*, Mélanie shared a bedroom with Toinon, while Luc slept in the adjoining room. But Toinon had been a baby then, and when Mélanie had leaned over the crib to tell her sister of Lucie's departure, Toinon had merely giggled back. Mélanie got into her own bed, sucked her thumb and fell into a restless sleep. She awoke to find the real world a continuation of her nightmare. The room glowed a luminous red. The walls were covered with leaping orange shadows. She stared, not moving a muscle, as her eyes searched the walls for an explanation. From outside the open window came a scream. Then another. She turned her head. Now she could hear the sound of other voices shouting and of cars coming to a stop. The baby began to cry. She wanted to get up, but she could not. Pulling the blankets up below her nose, she studied the weird patterns dancing over the wallpaper. She heard another scream. Toinon's cries grew louder. Mélanie forced herself to get out of bed and tiptoe over to the crib.

"Yes, I know. I know," she whispered, for she, too, was frightened.

She heard the siren of an approaching fire engine. She ran to the window and there, across the street, the old hotel was on fire.

She could see an interior staircase which wound past the vertical row of windows straight ahead of her. Framed by the window, a young woman in a white nightgown was rushing down the stairs. Flames rose from the floors above her, and suddenly from below a new flame leaped up. The woman turned, only to face the flames above. From the street came a man's voice: "Jump! Jump!"

Mélanie turned her back to the window and screamed: "Maman! Maman!"

The bedroom door burst open. Nurse came in and went straight to Toinon. In a firm voice she ordered Mélanie to stay away from the window. The room had an eerie, unearthly look as the progress of the fire across the street was reflected on its walls.

"I want Maman," Mélanie announced loudly.

"You know your mother's gone out to dinner."

"I want Lucie, then," she persisted, louder still.

"Get into bed!" Nurse commanded, taking a step towards her.

"Go away! Go away!" Mélanie shrieked. She rushed past the nurse, through the door and down the stairs, with no idea of where she was going. Standing at the foot, was Joël, the chauffeur.

"It's just a fire, little one," he said. "It will be over soon."

"Where is Lucie?" Mélanie asked for the tenth time that day.

An expression of stunned surprise came over Joël's face. "She's gone," he answered quietly.

"Mélanie, come back here," Nurse called from above.

Mélanie slowly mounted the stairs. She was sobbing uncontrollably. Nurse tucked her in bed, and still she sobbed. She felt certain she would weep until she died. Nurse closed the window and came over to kiss her, but she pushed the woman away and caught her own cascading tears with the tip of her tongue. Nurse closed the bedroom door behind her. Mélanie's throat ached, but her sobs went on and on.

The door opened noiselessly and Joël, six feet tall and huge, came to stand by the bed. "If you stop crying," he said, "and if you are very quiet, I'll show you a surprise."

Mélanie opened her arms. His heavy weight came slowly down and shook the bed. She put her arms round his neck and sobbed herself out against his bristled cheek. She was exhausted. The chauffeur lifted her up in his arms and carried her down the stairs. They went through the servants' dining-room; there was no one there. They walked up the back stairs, normally forbidden territory to the children, down a narrow corridor, and stopped before a closed door. Joël knocked. And Mélanie heard a familiar voice. "Come in!"

There, sitting up in bed, in a lovely pink nightgown, was Lucie! Joël deposited his load on the bed, smiled and walked out quietly. Mélanie let out a cry and threw her arms about Lucie's neck. She scrambled to get inside the sheets and nestle down. She felt at peace for the first time that day, until suddenly she heard a fearful sound.

"Oh, Lucie, don't cry!"

They hugged one another and giggled through their tears. Mélanie was happy and tired; and, as Lucie gently rocked her, she fell asleep.

When she awoke the next morning, she found herself in her own bed, and she did not know how she had got there. Looking out of the window, she studied the charred remains of the hotel. Over the grotesque, nameless shapes still standing, she had an uninterrupted view of the ocean. It was a deep blue, peppered with the dancing rays of the morning sun. It was going to be a lovely day.

After breakfast, Mélanie ran into the kitchen. She waved to Mme Babette, and called, "Good morning!" as she ran to the kitchen window. Cut low, almost to the ground, each window cradled a white window-box, topped with pink geraniums.

Mélanie jumped over one of them and found herself in the court-yard. Jean-Baptiste was opening the heavy wooden gate to allow the car, with Joël at the wheel, to get out.

She climbed on the mudguard and whispered, "Joël, where is Lucie now?"

"She's really gone this time. I put her on the train this morning. She was supposed to leave three days ago, you know, but Mme Babette and I kept her here until we were sure she had a place to stay in Paris. Well, she's got a nice room now, so she'll be all right." Then he added, "Maybe we'll go to see her when we get back."

Mélanie stepped off the mudguard. Joël got the car smoothly into gear and was gone. Jean-Baptiste closed the gate.

"Yes," Mélanie repeated to herself, "maybe we'll go to see her when we get back."

She walked slowly into the house. It was almost time to go to the beach, and Nurse would be looking for her.

THAT WAS THREE YEARS BEFORE. BRIGITTE did come the next day, as Mme Abbot had said she would. Brigitte, small, slim, quick, intelligent, was now so firmly entrenched as a member of the household that Mélanie had difficulty in remembering the days when she was not to be seen in some part of the house, polishing or dusting. She was always willing to be interrupted by a request for a story, a story she could never finish for laughing so.

Mélanie had now only a dim recollection of that rainy morning when she and Luc watched from their bedroom window to see two frail, uncertain figures approaching. Brigitte was accompanied by her mother and held an umbrella over them both. The old lady wore the long black native dress, with a white lace bonnet, pertly topping her grey head. They walked slowly, arms entwined, looking like a sombre, clumsily hewn statue hesitantly coming to life. Brigitte's mother, Mme Pomain, lived in a spotless, glowing little cottage by the harbour.

The children got to know her well, as passing by the tiny white fence that bordered her home, they could not resist pushing ajar the creaking gate that announced the arrival of visitors. Past a border of nasturtiums, through an arbour of wistaria, one came to the door of the cottage. The smell of recently baked bread or biscuit welcomed one into the combination parlour, bedroom and kitchen. And if children sat still and unsquirming on the four straw chairs, a mischievous light would spark Mme Pomain's fading blue eyes, a fleeting, toothless smile would wrinkle up her cheek, as she began an old legend of Brittany or told a tale of a sailor lost at sea, in the long ago when she was young.

As she sat with her hands folded on her knees and her feet propped on the rung of the chair, Mélanie's eyes circled this room which she loved, to notice anew the shiny wood-stove above which copper pans glimmered on their neat row of nails, the Quimper pitcher filled with marigolds, the only ornament on the brightly polished wood of the kitchen table. But it was the huge oak bed, taking up almost one entire wall of the small room, which fascinated her the most. It looked like a giant's coffin or the protruding hulk of a sunken vessel. It had an opening, covered by a red curtain, high beyond a child's reach.

When Mme Pomain had finished her story and risen to fetch her biscuits from the oven, Mélanie would ask if she might stand on the stepladder and peer into the bed. Without turning round, the old lady would exclaim, "But, *mon enfant*, you've already looked at it twenty times! It hasn't changed. It hasn't changed these forty years."

But she never failed to grant permission, and Mélanie, standing on a ladder, would part the heavy curtains and gaze at the red lining within, on which hung a crucifix and a round, crêpe-covered frame from which the late M. Pomain stared back at her, unsmiling and austere.

To lie in a bed like this, the curtains pulled tight, alone with one's dreams, hidden from the world outside, seemed to Mélanie

the height of beatitude; and when she grew up she would have a bed just like it; if only, as she fervently hoped, not every bed came with an unblinking photograph of a deceased Breton.

When the Abbots took their reluctant leave, Mme Pomain would slip into her sabots and walk with them to the creaking gate to bid them goodbye. When I am old, like Mme Pomain, Mélanie thought, I shall live like her in a Breton cottage, watering my flowers and putting out tin bowls of milk for the neighbouring cats. I shall live endlessly, toothless and grinning, hobbling on a wooden cane; I shall make biscuits for my grandchildren and listen to the sound of the sea hurling itself against the rocky shore; and I shall be happy and contented until the day I am lifted off the bed and carried down the winding dirt road to the chapel by the sea-wall.

IN SEPTEMBER, WHEN A GREAT MANY summer people had returned to their winter homes, M. Lachaise held only one class a day, in which all ages mixed as best they could. The remainder of the morning he was available for private lessons. Since he had long been a professional fencing champion, M. and Mme Abbot, together with Amaury's mother, who had a villa in Kerouan, decided to have their sons initiated into the mysteries of the sport. Luc and Amaury were to meet the instructor every morning at eight forty-five.

The beach was deserted then, as M. Lachaise, his back to the murmuring breakers, his eyes fixed on the two serious-faced boys, shivering before him, flourished his foil and blew his piercing whistle. The autumn breeze moved sharply around the rocky headlands and lifted papers and dust particles from the promenade to the height of a man. In bathing trunks and turtle-neck sweaters, the two boys bent their knees forward, brandishing their too-large foils, as goose pimples hardened the skin of their bare brown legs.

Mélanie, after some pleading and cajoling, succeeded one morning in getting permission to go to the beach and watch the fencing lesson. In a skirt and a woollen shawl, which Mme Babette had hastily thrown about her neck, she crossed the street and walked down the steps, cut steeply into the rock, which led to the far end of the promenade. As she made her way down, she could see three lone figures lunging at the sea, as if in defiance of the rising tide.

Some distance away, she sat on a humpy mound, the remains of a crenelated sandcastle. M. Lachaise, his helmet clasped in his curved left arm, his foil moving threateningly from a point in the sand to a less definable area of sky, shouted his disgust into the vast open space, as Amaury and Luc, standing side by side, bent their right knees and stretched their wavering left legs as far as they would go. When, at last, he was satisfied with the boys' progress, he nodded his head vigorously, then wiped his forehead with a clean handkerchief. Next came breathing exercises which M. Lachaise interrupted with horrified shouts of "Non! Mais non! Mais non!"

Mélanie got up, trudged across the sands and went home. It was not until Luc told her that he and Amaury were learning to use their foils, that she once again pestered her mother for permission to go to the beach right after breakfast. The mornings had turned perceptibly colder, so that M. Lachaise now held his class on the promenade, where the wall of the casino broke the force of the wind. The two boys moved backwards and forwards, touching their foils almost to their noses, then pointing them up, then down, as M. Lachaise issued orders in a foreign language: "*Prime! Quinte! Tierce! Quarte! Riposte! Flanconade!*"

To Mélanie these words sounded like lines from some archaic poem. Unable to resist their lure, she went to stand a few feet behind the boys and, waving an imaginary foil, she mimicked the instructor. In an exuberant state of trace, she bounded back and forth, until she found herself quite out of breath. She looked up to find M. Lachaise glowering at her. He held her with his glance for such a long time that Mélanie wondered if, perhaps, he had permanently lost his use of speech. He recovered it so suddenly that she took an involuntary step backward, while the sound of her name shattered the morning stillness. "Go, go at once! This is no place for female nonsense!"

Mélanie made herself as small as possible and, keeping close to the casino wall, she headed for home.

But the next day she was back. Posting herself at a discreet distance from the boys, she imitated their gestures as best she could. Again M. Lachaise screamed at her, "Mélanie, will you please go home! I'll see you in class, later. Later!"

But this time she paid no attention. She moved still farther away and went on with her exercises. That afternoon Luc told her that she was silly to come to the lessons.

"Fencing is an absolute bore," he assured her.

"I like it. I'm almost as good as you and Amaury."

"Well, good for you!" he retorted ungallantly. "I think it's a stupid sport. A lot of fuss for nothing. And who wants to end up like M. Lachaise, anyway?"

Her brother had a point there, but Mélanie dismissed it from her mind as irrelevant. She could not possibly grow up to be M. Lachaise, but she might, if she worked hard, become France's foremost woman fencer.

She attended the lesson the next day, and this time she came with a stick Jean-Baptiste had cut to her specifications. Amaury turned to look at her and smiled a guilty, admiring smile. But M. Lachaise seemed to be trying new tactics. His eyes avoided meeting hers, and he proceeded with the class as if she were transparent; or worse, non-existent. Day after day he continued to ignore her, while she concentrated on keeping her balance, her stick menacingly aimed at the sea. Amaury smiled at her as often as he dared, but Luc only shrugged his shoulders now and then to show his contempt.

When the two boys started fencing with each other, Mélanie found herself at a slight disadvantage. But, undaunted, she created an imaginary opponent for herself, and if her invisible foe bore a dwarfed resemblance to M. Lachaise, the coincidence only served to rekindle her zeal. One day, having plunged her stick into the adversary's chest, she had exultantly shouted, "*Touché!*" when M. Lachaise gripped her by the shoulders and shattered for ever the pleasurable aftermath of victory.

"Not that way," he said. "Move this shoulder forward. That's it. Now, try again."

Awed, she tried again.

"*C'est ça!* You've got it now!" The man's voice sounded almost joyful. Mélanie beamed into his tanned face. But the dark, hopeless look had returned.

"I don't know why I bother with you," he moaned. "I'm not being paid for a third pupil. And, anyway, why aren't you at home sewing?"

But Mélanie was glad to be counted among the living once again and, emboldened, she drew closer. She was further encouraged when Amaury, who had got in the habit of accompanying brother and sister to the foot of the stairs, even though his own home was at the opposite end of the beach, had whispered, "I like having you there. It makes me hate the lesson less."

Now that M. Lachaise had officially acknowledged Mélanie's

presence, he would occasionally focus his eyes on her and shriek, "She's got it! Mélanie's got it!"

This outburst always stopped the class for a few minutes, as the three surprised children stared at each other in silence.

A few days before the close of the month and, with it, the end of the lessons, M. Lachaise suggested that Mélanie be given a chance to show what she had learned. Handing her his own foil, he instructed her to stand facing her brother. Luc raised a scornful eyebrow but expressed no objection. Mélanie felt the weight of the unfamiliar sword and, her heart beating wildly, got into position. As sister and brother formally saluted each other, a look of intense surprise came over Luc's face. Mélanie dropped her arm and looked behind her. Her parents were coming towards them along the promenade. Her first thought was to run away, but she had been seen and it was too late.

"*Eh bien*," M. Lachaise exclaimed, "are you going to fence or not?"

Mélanie turned to Amaury, who nodded encouragingly. Once again she saluted her brother. But Luc was so unprepared for the intensity of her lunge, that he lost his footing and his sister scored a point. She glanced uncertainly at the instructor.

"Good," he said, "Now, Luc, pay attention."

As Mélanie resumed her position, such a fierce gleam came into her brother's eyes that she was unable to refrain from laughing out loud. Luc was visibly disconcerted, so that it was with joy, not unmixed with shame, that she called out, "*Touché!*"

Just then M. Abbot came up beside her and inquired, "What are you doing here?"

Mme Abbot let out a startled, "I had no idea!"

But Mélanie, flanked by the two boys, merely stared at her parents. Since no reply seemed to be forthcoming, M. Abbot cast an inquiring glance at the instructor. M. Lachaise pulled out his handkerchief and carefully wiped his brow before speaking. "I tried to send her home, but since she persisted in attending the class, I have given her some pointers. And she has a flair, a real flair for it."

"Is that so?"

Mélanie looked sheepishly at her perplexed father. A slow, warm smile lit his face and putting his hand on her shoulder, he added, "So, my daughter has a hidden talent?"

"But," Mme Abbot protested, "a girl . . ."

"There have been some excellent women fencers," M. Lachaise said somewhat dryly.

"Of course," M. Abbot agreed.

"May I stay then?" Mélanie asked.

"I suppose so," her father said. "You've gone this far, you might as well." And, taking his wife's arm, he addressed himself to the instructor. "We'll go along now and leave the three young champions in your care."

Luc shot his sister a disdainful glance, but she chose to ignore it. M. Lachaise blew his whistle and ordered Luc and Amaury to get in position. Mélanie stepped aside, and retrieving her stick, repeated to herself, "A flair, a real flair . . ."

In the ensuing days she was allowed to fence, first with Amaury, then with Luc; but the instructor was concentrating his attention on the boys, and Mélanie wondered if he had lost all hope of her ever becoming a fencer that France might be proud of. She spoke to no one of her uncertainty, but her enthusiasm was flagging. If the lessons had not been about to end, she would have given up.

On the final morning she thought of skipping class altogether; but when the time came, and Luc walked down to the promenade, she was not far behind him. M. Lachaise himself fenced with each boy in turn, then he made a little speech telling them that they had done well and that he was looking forward to instructing them further the following year.

Mélanie listened politely, but, certain that the words had not been intended for her, she was about to walk away when M. Lachaise thrust his foil into her hand and, without looking at her, said, "Here, keep it. You'll need it next summer."

She stared at him, dumb and unbelieving. Had she just been knighted, she could not have experienced a greater thrill. She felt as if she could easily rise from the ground and fly over the sea.

On the way home she held the foil in the crook of her arm, as though she were marching in a parade. When the three children reached the foot of the stairs, Amaury said, "Let's cross them."

"Why?" Luc asked.

"It's our last day."

Luc's only reply was a shrug of the shoulders, but Mélanie held out her sword and, while her brother looked on with pretended indifference, she touched blades with Amaury. Then pressing her foil to her chest, she proudly mounted the stairs.

MÉLANIE LOVED READING, AND THOUGH SHE preferred fairy tales to any other form of literature, she picked up anything that was legibly printed. She had been told many times that to sit hunched up in a chair, as she did, with no light and in poor posture, would certainly result in her being blind and hunchbacked. But her reading fed her imagination, and her excess musing, instead of being wafted like tumbleweed by the wind, could be stored for later use and refashioned into tales with which to keep her siblings awake at night. And, when she was sad or too excited to sleep, and her audience had been wooed away from her by Hypnos, she set off alone through mythical glens and wooded landscapes to discourse with elves and gremlins, or enslaved princes and distressed princesses. She had not heard of Peter Pan or Alice-in-Wonderland, but the tales of Charles Perrault she knew by heart. And when the Abbot children were given pocket money by aunts and uncles, it was seldom sweets they wanted, but a book. And going to the bookshop was a treat beyond compare.

It was quite a walk to the bookshop. One had to cut straight through the Luxembourg Gardens and walk on beyond them. As the glass door was pushed open, a light tinkling bell announced the arrival of new customers. At its sound, Mme Martin and her assistant would jerk their heads round to face the door, and then together they would call out warmly: "*Ah, bonjour, mesdames, messieurs!*"

Someone, or so it seemed, was always sitting in one of the straw chairs by the pot-bellied stove in the back of the shop; it was usually an old man browsing through a heavy, leather-bound volume. The Abbots walked directly to the children's book section to gaze in repressed excitement at the vast array of brightly coloured bindings. Nurse would sit herself down on a straight chair and patiently wait for them to make their selections.

Toinon always knew what she wanted—the latest issue of *Bécassine*; that funny little Breton girl who got herself triumphantly into, and then out of, the most embroiled situations. Toinon would take her book to the nearest chair and go through the profuse illustrations with an ecstatic look on her face.

If Claude, unaided, could find a book on dogs or cats, he, too, was content. But for Luc and Mélanie, the possibilities were enormous, and the choice a disturbing and difficult one to make. There was the whole series of the *Bibliothèque Verte*, all condensed classics; or the wonderful *Bibliothèque Rose*, which put out the moral melodramas of the Comtesse de Ségur. After some deep soul-searching, Mélanie would settle for one of these: "*Les*

Petites Filles Modèles," or *"Le Petit Bossu,"* or *"Les Malheurs de Sophie."* The pen and ink drawings of little girls in pantaloons and crinolines and of little boys half-hidden behind huge cravats, she found irresistible. Luc was inevitably the last to make up his mind. For him the colour and quality of the illustrations eventually outweighed the possible enticements of the text.

After the selections had been made, came the painful business of finding out from Mme Martin whether or not their choice was within their price range. Once or twice, but fortunately not often, a book had to be replaced on the shelf as a child bravely settled for second best. More often, however, if there was a slight discrepancy between the amount a child held in his open palm and the price of the book, Nurse graciously supplied the necessary number of extra sous or centimes. Each child carried his book with the greatest care, anxious to get home and show it to his parents and later to take it down to the kitchen for inspection by the servants.

If the children could read the books by themselves, they would sit in their nursery chairs in utter silence, but if the words proved too difficult, then their mother would read to them for a while after supper. Now and then, M. Abbot would sit in on the readings, quietly smoking in the arm-chair, and if something amused him, he would burst out laughing and start wildly searching for his handkerchief to wipe the tears away. Seeing their father doubled up with merriment would set his children to laughing, too, and if Mme Abbot spoke, trying to keep a straight face and say: "Wait! I have not finished the sentence," this would set them all off again into uncontrollable giggles. The young listeners were convinced that no one could read like their mother. She had the most beautiful voice in the world, and if M. Abbot sat in on the reading, this was the children's favourite hour.

the Fishers' huge Renault, between Frank and a young German nobleman of fifteen or so, who was a house guest of her host. She was grateful for the latter's presence, for being alone with Frank usually meant that she must muster all her patience and tact; and, playing the tacit rôle of Frank's girl, was one of her selves with which she never felt comfortable. It was an ordeal imposed by the adult world which offered no explanation but exacted unquestioning obedience. It took on various guises, such as a none-too-gentle urging to kiss some old family friend who might have down on her cheeks and a Delphic laugh; or a summons to change into a party dress and tight, slippery patent-leather shoes to curtsey before dinner guests, only to be chased back to the nursery a few minutes later.

While the car wound its way around the Étoile, Mélanie listened, or rather pretended to listen, to Frank's solemn, detached travelogue. In the absence of his parents, he was doing the honours of the city. In his neat short trousers and grey flannel jacket, he looked like a pint-sized squire, taking a foreign visitor on a tour of his estate. But instead of pointing at cattle and sheep with the butt end of a pipe, he was directing the gaze of his companion towards monuments and doorways, with the blade of his pocket knife. In between points of interest, he snapped the blade in and out of its silver case. The German boy, who was on holiday from his English school, grunted his appreciation but otherwise remained aloof, collected and monosyllabic.

It was Frank's birthday, and since Joël's services were required elsewhere, the Fishers' car had been dispatched to collect Mélanie. She had been surprised to find Frank and his guest in the car, but she could imagine how it had come about. Mme Fisher must have said, "Frank, dear, you *must* ask Mélanie to your birthday party. And wouldn't it be sweet if you went with the chauffeur to pick her up? I know how impatient you must be to see her again."

And Frank had probably looked down at his shoes, then, raising his head, had given his mother that pleasant, whatever-you-say smile of his, and the matter had been settled.

Mélanie glanced sideways at Frank. He was certainly being the perfect gentleman, carrying the burden of the conversation almost singlehanded and allowing no trace of boredom to show on his round, pale face. She felt a prick of conscience. She had not yet said a word, which was not in accordance with the lady-like behaviour expected of Frank's girl. She turned to the visitor and asked in her best party manner, "How long does Your Highness expect to be in Paris?" When the boy answered her with two beautifully enunciated words, she made a few comments on the difference between British and French schools, about which she knew almost nothing.

By the time the Renault came to a halt before the Fishers' house, she felt that she had conducted herself extremely well.

The luncheon was rather long, with M. and Mme Fisher self-consciously chatty with their eight young guests, and His Highness sitting in the place of honour, correct but uncommunicative. Only when the children found themselves alone in the upstairs nursery, did Mélanie really begin to enjoy herself. Frank had taken her aside to show her a picture album of himself in varying stages of growth but, now that they had had their *tête-à-tête*, she was free.

She lay down on her stomach, and with the assistance of several boys, she deployed Frank's tin soldiers on the rug. At the head of an army, planning her next battle, she was at ease once again.

The house guest, who was conspicuously older than the other children, sat on a chair, his legs crossed, reading the French edition of the *New York Herald Tribune*. But when Frank gave

Mélanie permission to use his brand-new cannon, she was so touched and excited that she rushed up to the young German and said, "Would Your Highness like to watch me shoot off this cannon?"

The boy looked perplexed but, putting down the paper, was kind enough to say that he would. Mélanie resumed her position on the floor and aimed. She shot down three hussars and a riderless horse, and Richelieu who happened to be standing nearby. The Cardinal's arm was knocked off by the blow, but there was no other damage. Frank dismissed the seriousness of the accident with a wave of the hand; so she aimed again. This time the bullet lodged itself in a boy's shoe. The recipient of the shot declared that Mélanie had thereby forfeited her turn. Acknowledging defeat, she not ungraciously relinquished the gun. A few minutes later His Highness was rolling his nice navy blue suit on the rug, preparing to shoot. He was a good marksman and had no trouble knocking down a whole regiment of cavalry. His victory was met with applause. This unexpected show of appreciation unloosened his tongue as well as the taut muscles in his long, aristocratic face.

When the Fishers came into the nursery an hour later, all the children were on the floor, the wooden fort was riddled with shots and half the tin soldiers were lying maimed on their backs. It had been a glorious afternoon, but the time had come for the guests to put on their coats and wait for their parents to claim them.

Frank looked as flushed and pleased as if the carnage they had left upstairs were a rite of spring instead of a massacre.

The Fishers' chauffeur was to drive Mélanie home, and while she thanked her hosts, the house guest made a mystifying request. "With your permission, I would like to accompany the young lady home."

Mme Fisher put her hand to her throat, and M. Fisher frowned in total incomprehension. Mélanie, however, had already been let in on the secret. The boy, while playing with the cannon, had split Napoleon in two and was anxious to replace him. After asking Mélanie if she knew where toy soldiers could be had and on being assured that she did, he decided to go with her and, on the way, pick up a new Napoleon and Cardinal.

"Then, I want to go, too!" Frank exclaimed, somewhat surprisingly.

"Should you not wait until all your guests have gone?" Mme Fisher suggested uncertainly.

Frank whispered to Mélanie, "Why does he want to go with you?"

"It's a surprise. A surprise for you."

"Oh," Frank said, and he let them go.

In the car the two children had some difficulty convincing the chauffeur that Mélanie was not to go straight home.

"Well," he said, looking sternly at them through the mirror. "If your parents find out, don't come crying to me for help."

Mélanie now wished it had been Joël at the wheel. He would not only have understood, but he could have told her whether she was being improper or doing the right thing.

With an assertive wave of the hand, His Highness said, "It's quite all right."

Mélanie shot a glance at him, then relaxed against the seat. Her companion was soon speaking freely of his brothers and sisters in Germany and his friends in England. When the car pulled up in front of a tiny shop, they threw open the door and hurried inside. The shop was so small that three people could hardly turn round in it. The proprietor sat on a stool below the unshaded bulb. The walls were lined with shelves upon which all the famous figures of history stood rigidly viewing one another.

After spotting the Cardinal, Mélanie remembered that she had left her purse at home. She touched the boy's elbow. "I'll have to wait to buy Richelieu, as I haven't any money. But I'll help Your Highness find Napoleon."

"My name is Heinrich," was his only reply.

"Oh," Mélanie said.

The old man who owned the store had not moved from his stool. When the boy asked him where Napoleon might be found, he pointed to a shelf behind his customers. Both turned round very carefully. The Emperor was standing amid his marshals, while Joséphine and Marie-Louise looked on in mute admiration.

"Should I get him Joséphine, too?"

"No, don't!" Mélanie cried and then, surprised by her own outburst, she added, "I think Frank would much prefer a marshal."

Napoleon I and Maréchal Ney came off the shelf.

"I'll take these two," the boy said, handing them to the old man, "and Richelieu."

"No!" Mélanie cried out again.

"Yes," His Highness retorted, with a commanding nod of the head.

Back in the car he said, "I consider it an honour to be taking the Cardinal to Frank, with your compliments."

"Frank," she began, "is not . . ." But she gave up. The situation was too involved. And, anyhow, it was all part of that grown-up world which the boy at her side would so shortly enter.

When she got out of the car in front of her apartment house, she shook the boy's hand. "Thank you, Heinrich."

As the car got into gear, the boy put his head out of the window and waved. "I'll tell Frank that his girl got safely home!"

Mélanie's hand went to her mouth.

"Oh, no," she moaned. "Frank is not . . ."

But it was too late. The car roared away, and the boy now waving from the rear window could not hear her.

was presiding over the road. Except for an occasional fight or minor accident, things were running smoothly. The gang, as the children called the third group, hovered about but did not interfere. One day, however, Mélanie felt uneasy. She discussed her anxieties with André. The gang, most of whom were in their early teens, were hanging around outside the park gate, near the foot of the road, watching. Some trouble was brewing, for, during the past week, instead of playing soccer nearby as they usually did, they merely stood, quietly gazing through the iron bars of the tall gate. Something ominous was surely afoot. But when the gang persisted in their strange behaviour day after day, Mélanie and André relaxed their watchfulness.

One afternoon, Mélanie stood at the head of the road, her scooter by her side, conversing with a friend. Some distance away André was tying on his roller skates. Part of Mélanie's attention noticed Luc starting off by himself, dreamily kicking his scooter down the slope. Engrossed in conversation, she was startled by a cry from André. She turned to see what had happened.

"Mélanie!" André shouted again, one hand pointing to the foot of the road. "Look!"

One by one, as though in slow motion, the gang was advancing along the inside of the gate. And, head bowed, Luc was making his solitary way towards them. Mélanie jumped on her scooter and tore down after him as fast as she could go. In a matter of seconds, the older boys had formed a semi-circle at the bottom of the road, and Luc was heading straight into it. When Mélanie reached him, her brother was standing stock still, one foot on his scooter, the other on the pavement. He was surrounded on three sides. She heard one of the boys issue a command. "Hand over the scooter and don't make a noise!"

Mélanie felt a shiver pass coldly through her.

"I won't," Luc answered firmly, standing intractable.

"Hand it over!" the boy repeated.

Luc made no answer. Mélanie slid down beside him.

"Get away from here!" a boy motioned her to the side.

"He's my brother. Leave him alone." Mélanie's voice did not sound as loud as she had thought it would.

"Hand over the scooter and be quick about it." The first boy was still addressing Luc.

"I won't," Luc repeated, imperturbable.

"Move back, Luc," Mélanie whispered.

"You stay out of this!" the second boy ordered. "This is man's business."

The first boy put both his hands on Luc's handle-bars, as if preparing to yank the scooter from under him. All at once Mélanie's mind cleared with the onrush of rage. She threw her own scooter down, stepped boldly in front of her brother and pulled at the aggressor's arms. Somewhere to her left another arm rose and hit her across the face. The blow unbalanced her and sent her sprawling across the road. She fell against the metal scooter and felt as if one side of her face had cracked in two. She heard Luc's outraged voice, "*Saligauds!*"

Then André's voice screaming: "Get out!"

Mélanie was too stunned to move. In a moment she felt Nurse's arms helping her up. Blood streamed down her cheek. She was ashamed to be crying. Several irate mothers and nurses were chasing the gang out of the park, but Mélanie's scooter had vanished.

For the next few days, the enemy gang played some way off, as though nothing had happened, but Mélanie and her friends had suffered a severe defeat, and they knew it. Not only had a scooter been stolen, but, by allowing the intervention of mothers and nurses, a serious rule of the code had been broken. This last had made it a doubly ignominious defeat; and the children realized that their days on the road were numbered.

When, a week later, a small car vanished as its owner had just stepped out of it, they knew the war was on in earnest. The enemy had the better weapons—age, numbers and cunning. It became too dangerous for a child to venture on the road alone. Mélanie organized two teams, so that as one went up the road, the other went down. This system made it possible to keep both ends of the road under perpetual surveillance. Still, vehicles went on mysteriously disappearing. The road was no longer a carefree stamping ground. It had become a centre besieged and in need of constant vigilance.

It was a cloudy afternoon when André noticed the gang massing itself anew outside the park gate. This time there was no mistaking the adversary's intention. The Members of the Road clustered together at the head of the incline, although no official meeting had been called. There was no need to discuss future plans. There would be no future. The handwriting on the wall was plain to read. They were outnumbered, out-foxed, and doomed. They waited, silent and defeated. They watched, unmoving, as the enemy re-formed its semi-circle and started its slow march towards them. The first drops of rain made an imperceptible sound on the tar. Soon, mothers and nurses would be calling their wards to shelter. It was the right weather for a moment such as this. The boy who had stopped Luc some weeks earlier took a position ahead of the others and addressed himself to André. "We've come to take it."

Head bowed and almost inaudible, André answered, "I know . . ."

Mélanie moved forward and faced the older boy. "It's yours."

She stepped back. It was her last official act. The sky had darkened, and the rain burst down on them.

"Let's go to the shelter," André suggested.

Speechless, the surrendering children stepped off the tarred road for the last time.

IT SO HAPPENED THAT THE ABBOTS' DAYS BY the road were to be terminated by yet another contrivance of fate.

For over a year Nurse had chosen to sit on a chair and pay her *dix* sous to the *chaisière* in this particular corner of the park because she had made a friend. Mme Durand was a dark, tense, frail-looking woman, who had married a dentist and produced a son and daughter. The Durand children were fifteen and twelve and considered the Abbots far too young to warrant their attention. This was most fortunate, for when they did condescend to show an interest, it was to exercise a rule of terror. Raised by a mother who was nervous and in poor health, they were self-centred, highly strung and cruel. They told stories so abominable that Mélanie had to put her hands to her ears in order not to hear them. They squirted water-pistols and carried darning needles with which to stab unco-operative playmates. They cheated at games and lost their tempers when anyone else did the same.

The Durands had once told Mélanie and Luc that they possessed an extraordinary and magnificent treasure, but they would only bring it to the park if the two Abbots first showed them how much silver they had hidden away at home. Trusting and credulous,

Mélanie and her brother brought their sparse savings the next day.

"Now will you show us your treasure?" they asked, all eagerness and faith.

"First," the Durand boy dictated, "you show us how much you've got. No, put it flat on your palm so we can see."

And as Luc and Mélanie exhibited their few sous and centimes, the older children quickly passed their hands over the out-stretched palms and ran off, smirking, with their victims' savings. Mélanie and Luc remained on the spot, stunned and aggrieved. How many months would it be before a kind aunt or uncle would find an opportunity to give them a franc or two? Gone for a long time, perhaps for ever, the hope of buying a coveted book or adding to their collection of tin soldiers.

But, by and large, the Durands left them alone, and since Mme Durand's chatter kept Nurse pretty well absorbed, the children could not object to a set-up which allowed them a certain amount of freedom to attend to their own affairs.

If life, on the whole, appeared to move to a pleasant rhythm, Mélanie, none the less, had grown to accept sudden, unexpected changes in its beat, and now and then a startling, inexplicable dissonance in its harmony.

One day soon after the road surrender, Nurse announced to her charges that she was moving to the other end of the park, and four faces looked up at her in speechless astonishment.

They walked across the Luxembourg Gardens, past the Senate and the pond, and up the terrace stairs. Beneath a white stone statue of Queen Mathilde, Nurse pulled out a chair and sat down. The children stood about her for a while in the hope that she might vouchsafe them some explanation. But Nurse was, with great concentration, taking her embroidery out of its cloth bag, and, realizing that no further information was forthcoming, they moved off to survey their new playground.

There was no tarred road here, but there was a row of statues to hide behind and a bandstand where once a week they might hear a military concert. They went to stand by the stone balustrade of the terrace, from which they had a view of the pond, the Medici Palace, and across to the opposite terrace, behind which lay their old hunting ground.

They had left their friends, and this was the worst disappointment to get used to. They took what consolation they could in that the lie of the land, even though unfamiliar, appeared to have its advantages.

One did not question adult decisions and movements, but only the most phlegmatic child remained incurious. Within an hour of their arrival in their new surroundings, the children had the answer to their unspoken question. A handsome man in a grey suit and top coat, with sleeked-down brown hair and dancing blue eyes, pulled up a chair and sat down next to Nurse. The children had seen him once or twice before and recognized him. He was Mme Durand's husband, the dentist.

Mélanie, Luc, Toinon and Claude hovered about at a discreet distance to watch the couple and figure out what they were to make of this. M. Durand did not stay long. After his abrupt departure, Nurse went on sewing as though this was an ordinary day and there was nothing strange in her being here, in a foreign place, her four charges displaced and companionless.

The next afternoon, the children followed their nurse across the park and waited restlessly about to see if the man would come again. He appeared, smiling and self-assured, and stayed a little longer. The couple spoke agitatedly in half-whispers, and whenever a child came near, Nurse waved him away, telling him to run along. There was a steely urgency in her voice which allowed for no appeal. The children kept their distance, and the day was longer than a day had a right to be.

On the third day the children knew their exile to be permanent. Nurse called them to her and introduced them to the dentist.

"This is M. Durand," she said, as if it were quite natural for her to be sitting with him, here, after having sat for a year or more with his wife at the opposite end of the park.

"I've brought you each a present," M. Durand announced, as he pulled some chocolate cigarettes from his breast pocket. This was the infallible sign. Such a premeditated act of courtship could mean but one thing. He had moved into their lives to stay. Even a child untutored in the intricacies of social intercourse can read adult posturing with the speed of light.

The dentist came every day and stayed about an hour, except

Wednesdays and Saturdays when he stayed all the afternoon. Unmoved and unblinking, Mathilde, Queen of France, glimmered whitely in the sun while the lovers, seeking her shadow, moved twin chairs about her broad base.

A new era had begun for the Abbot children. They were never to return to their familiar haunts by the tarred road. This elevated, dust-strewn expanse of ground, running parallel to the Boulevard St. Michel, was now their home. Faced with the inevitable, they explored in earnest. They not only examined the contours of the land and the possibility it afforded for games, but they studied the faces about them to sort the regulars from the accidental trespassers; and, among the former, examined the ground for possible overtures of friendship. But this last survey offered little promise. Most of the children seemed to be mere infants. At the other extreme were the students who erupted at about three o'clock in the afternoon from the confines of the Sorbonne. The latter were fun to watch, for they were a rowdy, busy, mischievous lot; but even this source of entertainment palled in time. The elder Abbots found partial comfort in that Claude had made a friend. Michel was an only child, Claude's age, and the two boys seemed happy to have found each other. When their capacity for mutual play was exhausted, Michel would attach himself to the Abbot clan and tag behind, as if tied to them by an invisible thread.

The first week in their new habitat passed slowly for Mélanie, Luc and Toinon. It was not until ten days later that something happened to give them hope of better things to come. They were fascinated to see workmen not far from the park gate dig four holes and drive poles into them. The children were told that an outdoor cinema would open soon. This was, they knew, something that existed nowhere else and, by some stroke of good fortune, it was to happen right here, within the boundaries of their allotted freedom.

The cinema turned out to be quite different from anything they had envisaged, but it was also far better. The four poles supported a huge, elongated box which looked somewhat like an outsize coffin and stood about seven feet high. A small screen was mounted at one end of the rectangular box. A rope attached to metal rods encircled this strange contraption. A few rows of folding chairs were lined up inside the roped-off enclosure, and for the privilege of sitting on these, it was necessary to pay an admission fee. But one could stand outside the rope free of charge. There were two shows a day, and if small children wished an unobstructed view, they had to take their places well ahead of time. The young Abbots always missed the first showing, since they were at home having lunch at that hour, but they were always on hand for the second, lined up against the rope fifteen minutes early. The films were usually documentaries on plant and animal life and one of Charlie Chaplin, known to all Frenchmen simply as *Charlot*. One blond, wiry, middle-aged man handled the whole performance. He put up the rope, unfolded the chairs, manned the projector and took the fees. The Abbots were soon on casual, friendly terms with him. They called him M. l'Ingénieur in deference to his manifold skills; and they plied him with so many questions that once he came to his post ahead of his usual time so that he could show them the back of the screen and enlighten them on the mysteries of the projector.

Most of the children who were escorted to the park had a closer surveillance than that which the Abbots now enjoyed and were not allowed to dally around *le cinéma*. Old men and women sat inside, while the standing audience was made up for the most part of students from the University. The latter proved the more responsive spectators, providing the claque, the inevitable boos and cat-calls, the laughter and the witty asides. One of these was a young man of nineteen years or so, with blond curly hair, large, guiltless brown eyes set in a long, soft, amiable face. His name was Jacques. The children had discovered this one day when the projector had broken down and the student had volunteered to give M. l'Ingénieur a hand. Between the two of them they managed to get the projector to work again, amid the booing and jeers of the students. Luc had politely inquired what had gone wrong, so the two men demonstrated what had happened and how they had repaired it. The explanation was followed by introductions all round. From that day, Jacques, and eventually all the students, addressed the now for ever anonymous concessionaire, as M. l'Ingénieur. Jacques soon became a friend, and lined up every day beside the eldest Abbots. Claude and Michel seldom attended the performance because they got too restless to see it through to the end. When the film was over, Jacques took the children for a walk or played games with them. If he got tired, for he was not an athletic type, he sat on a bench and told them of the latest pranks the students had tried out at the Sorbonne.

One day a frown formed itself upon his normally untroubled face, and he asked Mélanie how it was that such well-bred and neatly dressed children played about the park, unattended and unwatched.

"We'll show you," Mélanie said eagerly.

"*Viens voir!*" and Luc pulled at his sleeve.

They led him to a spot against the stone wall where Nurse was not likely to see them. It was a bright, glaring, sunny day. Luc pulled a mirror from the pocket of his short trousers and said, "Watch!"

He aimed the glass so that a bright circular patch of light shone against the statue. He moved it carefully until it danced on Nurse's lips and the tip of M. Durand's nose. The lovers had their arms about each other, oblivious to the world. Of themselves they were scarcely noticeable. Two feet away from them, a woman was breast-feeding her baby. With her back to the mother, an old woman was spitting cherry stones into a paper bag. Across the way, against a tree, a teen-aged girl was holding her small sister, urging her to urinate. Two boys were rolling on the ground, fighting in front of a group of students balancing on the back of chairs. One of these was trying to slip a pencil down the v-neck of a girl's sweater. No doubt, out of sight but not far away, an old man was sitting conversing with death, and another pair of lovers stood with their arms entwined.

As the patch of light moved up to her eyes, Nurse made an annoyed movement of the hand, as if pushing a fly away.

"Stop it, Luc," Mélanie whispered.

The children made a conspiratorial dash away from the wall, dragging Jacques with them. When they reached their favourite bench, Mélanie explained, "He's a dentist."

"And he's married," Luc added.

That was the sum of their knowledge.

"How long has this been going on?" Jacques assumed a parental tone.

"Oh, about a month," Mélanie guessed.

"Have you told your parents?"

"Of course not."

"I think you should."

"Then we'd be tattle-tales," Luc said.

The Abbots were thoroughly trained in the children—servant code. If you did not tell tales on the servants, they would not tell tales on you. Codes were a matter of simple logic.

"Nurse would be in a real mess if we told," Mélanie thought out loud.

"It's nice," Toinon added.

Mélanie knew what her sister meant. They had never enjoyed as much freedom before. Now no one told them how far they could stray, when to play or when to rest; no one bothered to make them blow their noses or pull their socks up. It was the most benign jurisdiction they had ever been subject to.

"Well, I don't know about this," Jacques mused. "She's paid to take care of you. She should keep her romancing for her days off."

"He only stays an hour," Mélanie said, searching for attenuating circumstances, "except for Wednesdays and Saturdays."

Jacques shook his head. "It's not right." This was as close as the children had ever seen him to suffering from any form of mental anguish. "I'll have to think it over," he added, a note of irritation in his voice. It was quite obvious that he did not relish having to grapple with ethical challenges.

The children were relieved when several weeks went by during which Jacques did not raise the subject again.

One late afternoon, as they were hurrying home beside Nurse, before the threatening clouds burst into a storm, they passed Mme Durand and her two children walking hastily in the opposite direction. Nurse stiffened noticeably, then catching hold of Claude and Toinon, she said, *"Dépêchons-nous!"*

All five of them walked on without turning their heads. Mme Durand, too, gave no sign of recognition, but when the Abbots had gone past, the Durand children hurled a volley of abuse at them. Mélanie did not recognize the words; they were argot. All she knew was that they were vile and not for her to understand. It was an unpleasant moment, but it passed.

The next Wednesday, as the children were approaching the outer boundaries of the cinema, they noticed that Jacques and M. l'Ingénieur were carrying on a whispered conversation. When the two men saw them approaching, they raised their hands and gestured them to stay away.

"Pas aujourd'hui!" M. l'Ingénieur yelled.

The children halted, bewildered. Jacques came towards them.

"M. l'Ingénieur does not think you should see this film. There are things in it that are not meant for children."

Mélanie felt her muscles tightening with disappointment.

"Of course, if you had a nurse who knew her duty, you would not be seeing any of these films."

"Oh, Jacques!" Luc wailed.

"Ah, yes," Jacques replied philosophically, "it's true. It's just because you are being neglected that you're seeing all this rubbish."

Neglected? Mélanie had not thought of herself as neglected before. The sound of the word gave her a peculiar, uneasy feeling. She had heard of neglected children, but she had never entertained the possibility of one day becoming one herself. She pictured them barefooted and dirty, with huge hungry eyes, sleeping in horses' stalls. In books children were often neglected, but in life had she ever seen any? Could this be the start of the road to hunger and total abandonment? The thought disturbed her.

"M. l'Ingénieur does not think," Jacques went on without hurrying, "that most of the films shown can harm you. But this one he wouldn't show to his own children, if he had any. I don't know, of course. But I daresay he's right . . ."

"But I have a father and mother!" Mélanie interrupted. That word "neglected" would give her no peace.

"Yes, well, they wouldn't let you see any of these films either. I suggest you do what the engineer says and stay away from the films until he tells you that you can watch them again."

The five of them sat down on a bench. Jacques leant his head on his hands. He was thinking in his usual ruminant fashion. Mélanie tried to imagine herself sleeping in a stall, feeling cold and hungry. She saw the huge black eyes of her brothers and sister, and something close to panic stirred in her. She shook Jacques' sleeve. "We are not neglected!" she cried. "Maman and Papa would never abandon us. Never! They wouldn't let Claude cry and sleep in a stable!"

Claude looked up at her. "Oh, Méli, no!"

Mélanie threw her arms about her younger brother, as he shuddered against her. Tears welled up in her eyes. Claude clung tightly to her. Toinon slipped down from the bench and, putting her arm round her sister's shoulder, asked gently, "What's the matter?"

Jacques stared at them uncomprehending. "You're not all going to cry just because you can't go to a film?"

There was no answer. Luc was watching his sisters. Claude saw nothing because he had buried his face against Mélanie's chest.

"What a family!" Jacques railed. "*Alors*, what am I supposed to do, ask the engineer to change his programme for your special benefit?"

The vehemence of his tone shook them back into a semblance of serenity.

"No," Luc assured him. "We won't go."

"No, we won't," Toinon echoed.

"*Bien*," Jacques sighed. His voice was softer now. "Then I won't go either. We'll do something together. Perhaps we could go to my father's shop for tea. He's been wanting to meet you. He says he can't believe that I've saddled myself with a family of four children!"

"Your father is a photographer?" Luc asked.

"Yes, his photography shop is right here, on the boulevard."

"Does he put a black cloth on his head and say, 'look at the birdie?'" Luc asked again.

"Yes, he does. He might even take your picture if you're good. . . . Wait, here," he added. He rose abruptly and ran out through the park gates.

The children waited. Mélanie no longer felt neglected. M. l'Ingénieur was looking out for their best interest, and Jacques' father wanted to have them for tea. That night her mother and father would kiss her goodnight, as usual.

Jacques returned a few minutes later, quite out of breath.

"I spoke to Father. It's all arranged. We'll go over in half an hour."

"Will we have tea in the shop?" Luc wanted to know.

"In the back of the shop," Jacques corrected. "But my father will show you all his equipment and the darkroom, if you like."

"Yes, and I want to take a picture," Luc announced.

Jacques smiled and ruffled the boy's hair. They all rose from the bench and automatically started for a walk. Mélanie took his hand. He was giving up the film to be with them. Perhaps he was young to be a father, but being a student at the University gave him an aura of glamour and authority.

"Is your father an old man?" Toinon asked.

"Not so old. But he's the nicest father a man could have. In a year or two, I'll be working with him in the shop."

"You'll be a photographer?" Luc asked, looking up at the young man with reverence.

"Yes, it's a good *métier*," Jacques replied, obviously pleased with himself and the whole idea.

"And your mother, where is she?" Mélanie interrupted.

"She's dead. She died a long time ago."

He had already told her this, but she had forgotten. Dead, like her French grandmother and grandfather whom she had never known. It was hard to imagine not having a mother. The war of 1914—*la Grande Guerre*, as it was still called—had made the death of fathers a familiar reality, if still unimaginable. A great many children who played in the Luxembourg had no father. But all of them had mothers. You could see them knitting or sewing, still in their widows' weeds. The war had been fought, won and done with by the time Mélanie was born, but it was more real to her than last year's *Tour de France*, more real even than her visit the year before to the United States. It weighed on her still, as it did on every Frenchman alive, for its implacable hand was visible everywhere. There were Oncle Guy and Oncle Didier, first cousins and childhood playmates of her mother, who had been killed in their full youth. And then there was "that lady," as the children called her, for they had not yet dared to speak to her, who wheeled her husband about in a baby carriage. All that remained of him were his head and torso. Fathers swollen twice their size by gas walked their offspring on Sundays. Men in wheelchairs, feeding the birds, were a common sight. Two of the park guards had wooden legs. Men with a black patch over one eye, men minus one or two arms were daily reminders of a brush with death.

Death was not a nebulous word that one could leave out of one's vocabulary until some very distant future. Death was ever present. But losing one's mother, to Mélanie, was almost inconceivable. She pressed Jacques' hand. Still, he looked happy, serene and well cared for.

"Papa wants time to put on the table-cloth and get some *pâtisseries*," he was saying.

"How far is it to your father's shop?" Mélanie asked. Some indefinable uneasiness had retaken possession of her.

"Oh, it's quite near here; on the boulevard."

"Wonderful!" Luc was hopping with anticipation.

"I'm tired," Claude announced, but no one paid any attention to him.

"Let's go this way." Mélanie pulled Jacques' hand. She wanted to circle the statue to see if Nurse showed signs of anxiety. They halted a safe distance away. M. Durand had his arms tightly clasped about the nurse's waist. Her head rested on his shoulder. The children were on their own.

"Well, it's four-thirty, let's go," Jacques said, and they all walked quickly away, as far as the garden gate. As they reached the pavement, the uneasy feeling returned to plague Mélanie.

"We'll cross here," Jacques said.

Mélanie stopped abruptly. "We can't cross the street," she told him.

"We have to," Jacques replied, pulling her hand. "The shop's on the other side."

"You didn't tell us that!" Mélanie shouted.

"But it's not far. See, you can see it over there!"

Mélanie heard her mother's voice, speaking from somewhere within her: You are never to cross a street, under any circumstance, unless accompanied by me, your father or Nurse. If you get lost, don't ask a stranger, ask a policeman to take you home.

"We can't cross the street." This time her voice was firm.

"Why not?"

"It's forbidden," Mélanie answered, and turned back towards the park.

"Let's straighten this out." Jacques showed signs of irritation. "We'll sit down and discuss it."

Solemnly, they filed back into the park and sat down on the nearest bench. Jacques addressed himself to Mélanie. "What's forbidden?"

"To cross a street with anyone but Maman, Papa or Nurse."

"*Tiens!*"

"If we are lost," she went on, "we can ask a policeman but not a stranger."

Jacques started to speak very slowly, as though she were a hard-of-hearing alien. "I—am—not—a—stranger. We—are—going—to—visit—my—father. He's—a—nice—man. He—won't—harm—you. I—won't—harm—you. We'll—just—have—afternoon—tea—and—come—back."

It sounded most reasonable to Mélanie. She was quite sure that Jacques' father was a nice man. She had looked forward to meeting him. But her mother had said not once, but many times, never to cross the street.

"I don't know," Mélanie sighed. This was very difficult. "Maman said never."

"What do you think?" Jacques asked her brother.

Luc spoke like a somnambulist: "You are never to cross a street, under any circumstances, unless accompanied by me, your ..."

He was about to repeat the whole thing, when Mélanie interrupted hastily, "We know, Luc."

"Under any circumstances," Jacques muttered to himself.

"Never," Toinon interposed firmly.

"I'm hungry," Claude was getting restless again.

"Go wee-wee," Mélanie ordered.

"Come with me, Méli," he cooed.

"Luc will go with you."

There was great confusion in her mind. She listened again and again to her mother's voice. It was clear enough.

"*Zut*," Luc swore, but he got up just the same and disappeared with Claude behind a tree.

"It's complicated, but the circumstances are a bit unusual. We wouldn't be doing anything actually wrong," Jacques said.

"I don't know," Mélanie replied. Her mother had not said anything about such an eventuality.

"I'll go and tell my father that we're talking things over and will be a little late." Jacques got up and vanished from the park.

When Luc returned, his sister asked him "What do you think?"

"Maman says not under any circumstances."

"What are we going to do?" Toinon asked.

Luc shrugged his shoulders.

"I think we had better refuse. Politely," Mélanie suggested.

"Perhaps," Luc, too, looked troubled. "Should we ask M. l'Ingénieur?"

"He's busy."

"I'll go and see." Luc walked away.

Jacques came back panting. "Father says he quite understands your difficulty. He suggests that we go and ask your nurse if she'll let you come."

"Oh no!" Mélanie exclaimed.

Luc was approaching with M. l'Ingénieur at his side. The latter spoke to Jacques, "What's all this about tea and crossing streets and your father?"

Jacques explained the situation.

"That hussy!" and the engineer made a movement of the head in the general direction of the nurse. "Well," he added, "you've got yourselves quite a problem there."

"I know," Jacques said faintly. "I can't force the children against their better judgment."

"No, you can't do that. I think *Monsieur votre père* has the answer. The children should ask their nurse if it's all right."

"Oh no!" the children pleaded. "She must not find out about the two of you and the cinema, or we'll never see either of you again."

"True," was the engineer's reply.

"Don't you think they could cross the street just this once?" Desperation was again discernible in Jacques' voice. "My father went out to buy *pâtisseries* . . ."

"I know. It's a shame. But it's obvious that these children are not used to disobeying. Better let it go this time."

Mélanie felt relieved. The engineer was siding with her mother.

"I'm sorry about your father," she faltered. "We would like to meet him. Would you thank him for us? Perhaps . . ."

But Jacques was running out of the park again. Mélanie

suddenly felt tired. Her brothers and sister looked weary, too.

"Come with me," the engineer said. "You can wait for me while I put my equipment away."

M. l'Ingénieur in his workman's clothes, his head down and his hands in his pockets, walked ahead of the sad little procession. Back at his post, he started to dismantle the projector, while the four children sat down on the folding chairs and watched him. Jacques came back, carrying a small box of cakes. He dropped it in Mélanie's lap. "My father says he understands. He sends his regards."

When the engineer finished with his chores, he pulled up a chair, and for a while they all sat in silence, nibbling at the cakes.

"Well," the engineer finally spoke, "they're pretty good young ones."

"My father was so disappointed," Jacques answered.

"Another time perhaps," Luc ventured timidly.

"Maybe some day he could come to the park and have tea with the children here."

"It's not likely that he can leave the shop," Jacques muttered.

"Will you convey our regrets and our gratitude?" Mélanie said very formally.

"I shall," Jacques replied despondently.

"Well, we'll arrange something," the engineer added. "I'd like to meet *Monsieur votre père* myself."

"Oh, and me, too!" Toinon joined in.

But they were never to meet Jacques' father, for an incident which took place a week later changed the course of their lives once more.

velvety, windless, and intoxicating. The Abbots were crossing the park on their way home. Nurse was holding Claude by the hand, walking slowly and patiently, while the older children absently lagged behind. Suddenly, Nurse stopped. The children looked up. Mme Durand was coming towards them, her two offspring staring. All three looked like birds of prey poised on an invisible rocky ledge, gauging place and distance before taking the swift plunge towards battle, food and satiation. There was a fraction of a moment when everyone stood stock still.

Then the Durand girl made the first move. She took a few quick steps nearer Nurse, then stuck out a long flat tongue. Mélanie had seen boys on the street do this, boys from another world, but a girl . . . She lost the thread of her thoughts, for the word "bitch" suddenly resounded loudly through the air. She could not make out from whence it had come. She noticed that the two women were now face to face. From that moment on, things happened so fast that Mélanie lost track of the sequence of events. From one or the other of the women came an animal scream. Two hats fell on the ground, as, moaning, the rivals were now fiercely tugging at each other's hair. Jungle cries wrenched the air. A crowd started to form, while the Durand children danced helplessly about the contestants. But when the two women became figures writhing and rolling on the sandy floor, something snapped in Mélanie's mind, and all her senses returned to her. She looked at her brothers and sister who were staring, mute and pale.

Then she took Toinon and Claude by the hand and, with a jerk of the head, signalled Luc to follow her. "We're going for a walk," she announced. Surely this was not a sight for the younger ones to witness. She led them towards the pond. "I'll tell you a story," she said, "about a little boy who wanted a boat to sail on the pond, here. But he didn't want to ask his parents, for they were very poor . . ."

Her mind was racing. She had no idea what she would say next, but she had to go on and keep her siblings' eyes concentrated on the pond.

"Well, one day, this little boy, whose name was Coco, had an idea . . ." She wondered what would happen now, whether Nurse would shortly be coming to look for them, or if she had better plan to head for home. "He knew that the village carpenter kept his wood in an abandoned shed. So Coco decided . . ."

They walked once round the pond. She must concentrate; her story-telling was meandering. ". . . and he ran and ran as fast as he could go. . . ."

A booming male voice interrupted her. "Eh! *Attendez, les enfants!*"

The children looked back. A plump, blue-eyed, uniformed guard was running after them. It was M. Guitard.

"Come," he said, "I'm taking you home."

Trustingly, they fell in step with him.

"*Quel scandale!*" he wailed. "*Quel scandale, alors!*"

But the children kept silent. He slowed down his pace, so that they wouldn't have to run. After a while, he started telling them about the bees he kept in a corner of the park; and soon the children were chatting, too, asking him all kinds of questions.

As they neared the gate, Mélanie asked, "What are you going to tell Maman?"

"That," he answered, "will be between your mother and me. You children just forget the whole thing." Prodding him was useless. He would not say any more.

Standing before their front door, the children felt tense and uneasy. The guard pressed the bell. Brigitte opened the door. When she saw the park guard and four sober little faces gazing back at her, she flew down the corridor shouting: "Madame, oh, madame!"

Mme Abbot hurried into the hall. "What has happened?"

"Everything is all right," the guard answered quickly, and, taking off his cap, he added, "I believe, if Madame will permit me, that we should have a little talk."

"Certainly," and Mme Abbot ushered him into the living-room where she at once closed the double glass doors.

Brigitte pushed the children ahead of her into the nursery. She helped them shed their hats and coats, then passed a flannel over their hands and faces.

Luc and Mélanie ran out into the corridor, unmindful of the maid's entreaties. They pressed their ears up against the living-room doors. A curtain stretched taut across the glass prevented them from seeing in. They could distinguish the male from the female voice, but not the words. They retreated into a corner of the passage and waited. The doors opened. Mme Abbot shook hands with M. Guitard. On his way to the front door, the guard patted the two children on the head, without a word.

"Now run along," Mme Abbot said. "It's time for your baths."

For the rest of the day, the children did not see Nurse and they meekly obeyed Brigitte's admonitions.

The next morning, Nurse, crisp and efficient in her white indoor uniform, came to wake them as usual; but that afternoon it was their mother who took them for a walk in the park. She seemed preoccupied and not her normally cheerful self. She appeared to be walking with a purpose, and her children were surprised to find themselves pacing up and down a little-used path.

"I am going to meet someone," she said at last, "and when he comes, I want you to run ahead of me to play and not disturb us until we are through."

Mélanie had no time to ask herself who the stranger might be,

for she had just noticed a handsome, dapper man approaching
them at a leisurely pace. She was struck once again by the
unfathomable spider-web world in which adults seemed to move.
What was her mother doing, keeping a rendezvous with the
dentist in this deserted side path?

Durand bent hastily over Mme Abbot's hand. When it was released, she made a shooing movement at her staring children. Mélanie promptly turned round. For an unspeakably frightening moment, she expected to see the grown-ups go in search of a statue, with two empty chairs at its base. She pulled at her hoop. She had no desire to play. Her mother's voice, sharp, cold, commanding, broke the awkward silence. "Well, M. Durand, I believe you and I have something to talk about."

They would not be looking for a statue! The world was not topsy-turvy after all. Mélanie swung her wooden stick, gave her hoop a hard blow and flew after it.

The interview lasted about twenty minutes. The dentist disappeared up the path, without glancing at the children. Mme Abbot's voice had resumed its warm, cheerful tone. "Well, children, how would you like to see the guignol?"

The next day Nurse woke them in the morning and fed them their lunch and dinner, but this time it was Brigitte who accompanied them to the park. They managed to talk the maid into sitting down near the cinema. When they had played quietly for a while and felt sure that she was thoroughly engrossed in the novel she had brought along, they went off in search of Jacques. After locating him, they informed him of the new turn of events. The student said he was glad to hear of it and that things would be better from now on. But the children doubted this. They had no way of knowing whether or not they would be seeing their new friend again, and this saddened them. They did not go to the film that day, but when the show was over they signalled M. l'Ingénieur to meet them behind the bandstand. He hurried over, mystified. They told him the events of the past few days and confided their uncertainty as to the future. In two more weeks they would be leaving for Kerouan, but until then they did not know to which part of the park they would be taken. This was almost a farewell. M. l'Ingénieur mumbled stupidly, "Send me a postcard." Then he kissed each child, hastily wiped his eyes, and, turning his back, walked away.

The following days were most unsettling. Mme Abbot and Brigitte took turns walking the children, while Nurse stayed at home.

One day Luc overheard his mother speaking to her husband. "It will soon be time for the children to have a governess. They are not learning any languages. . . ."

Luc and his sisters discussed this latest intelligence at supper time. Their fate was in the balance, and the uncertainty of it threw them into a turmoil. They agreed to take their problem to Joël at the first opportunity.

The next morning it was Brigitte who woke them. Nurse was nowhere in sight. Mélanie tore down the stairs and ran out of the kitchen door, across the courtyard and into the garage. Joël was washing the car. When she had put all her questions to him, he leaned against the bonnet, folded his arms across his chest and answered her. "As far as Nurse is concerned, she was fired and she left." He shrugged his shoulders. He had never liked Nurse much. "Brigitte will take her place for the moment, and Jeanne, a niece of Mme Babette, is coming to do the cleaning. This will give Madame time to find the right person."

"But languages . . ." Mélanie cut in.

"Ah, yes, languages! Well, I don't care much for the idea myself. Let's hope she's French at any rate. But nothing will happen until we get back from Kerouan, because Brigitte is coming with us."

Mélanie returned to the nursery greatly relieved. She passed the information on to Luc and Toinon. Her brother drew a comforting conclusion. "It's not so bad, especially as I can make Brigitte do almost anything I want."

Toinon and Mélanie exchanged a glance. The maid's preference for Luc might be a good thing after all.

home and Nurse was gone, so Mélanie picked up her doll and tip-toed noiselessly into the living-room. Nicholas, his eyes fixed on his galloping fingers, seemed not to have noticed her entrance. She held her breath and made her way to the piano. Once safely under it, she sat down, firmly clasping Nadine to her chest.

Whatever the young man was playing, it was very sad. Mélanie felt the sadness grip her stomach and constrict her heart. She was now sorry that she had come. The music reminded her of some of the songs her mother sang.

When Françoise's parents came to dinner, Mme Abbot would often sing while Mme de Béard accompanied her on the piano. If the children were in bed, they could still hear their mother's rich full voice; and sweet was their resistance to sleep those evenings. But there were times when Mélanie wanted to jump out of bed and run to her mother to beg her to stop, for she could not endure the mysterious anguish which came into her voice when she sang a dirge or a lament. Mélanie liked to picture Mme de Béard—she was Tante Hélène to the children—with her auburn hair and light, translucent skin, seated at the piano and Mme Abbot standing beside her, making a handsome tableau in their evening gowns, as M. Abbot and Oncle Paul listened from their arm-chairs, each half-hidden behind a blue spiral of smoke. Even though Mélanie sensed the relaxed inti-macy of these evening concerts, she could only give herself whole-heartedly to them when the songs her mother sang were gay and fast and ended on a high, joyful note.

Mélanie was about to crawl out from under the piano, when the music suddenly ceased, and Nicholas peered down at her. Upside down, his face looked like a misshapen, pock-marked balloon. She turned her head away, and when she looked again, the balloon was gone.

From above the instrument, Nicholas asked, "Did you like that?"

"No," she said.

"That's a pity. I think it's very beautiful."

Mélanie did not comment.

"What are you doing here?" he asked again.

She made no reply.

"Aren't you supposed to be getting ready for the park?"

"It's raining."

"I see."

The conversation might have ended there if, after a long pause, he had not ventured another question. "Are you crouching down there because you love to hear the piano?"

Before she could prepare her answer, he asked again, "Because you like music?"

"Nadine does," she said.

"Who is Nadine?"

"You met her after Christmas, remember?"

"No. I'm afraid not. Who is the young lady?"

Mélanie got up and went to stand by the piano bench. "Here she is."

"Oh, it's Nadine, is it? *Bonjour*, Nadine."

He shook the doll's hand.

"Does Nadine really like the piano?"

"Oh, yes! It makes her feel all funny and squeezy inside."

"Squeezy?"

"Like a flower folding slowly before it dies."

"What?"

"Well, maybe more like a butterfly whose wings are beating against the glass, because he does not know that the window is shut."

"And that's how music sounds to you?"

"To Nadine," she corrected.

"I see. Does she tell you these things?"

"Yes. And she can talk to you, too."

"Are you sure?"

"Yes."

"Well then, Mademoiselle Nadine, do you suppose Mélanie would like to have a piano lesson?"

"No, but . . ."

"I know," Nicholas broke in. "Nadine would. Is that it?"

Mélanie grinned.

"Well, we'll have to see about that. Her fingers seem a bit short for this keyboard."

Mélanie's spirits sank. She had not thought of that.

"Perhaps you could teach her to dance?" she suggested, opening a new avenue of hope.

"To dance? Why, heavens, that's not my line at all!"

The avenues were fast closing down; she tried another tack. She held her doll up for inspection. "Do you think she's pretty?"

"Very pretty. I believe she looks a bit like you. Except for those blue eyes." But he was no longer looking at the doll. He had begun to flip through his music sheets, as if trying to decide what to play next.

"*You* have blue eyes," Mélanie reminded him.

"Yes, I do. But we haven't time to talk about me," and turning to face her, he asked, "Wouldn't Nadine like a ride in her carriage?"

Mélanie realized that she was being asked to leave. Hurt by the abruptness of the dismissal, she backed away; but before leaving the room, she hastily dropped Nadine on to the sofa.

When Nicholas had gone, she went back into the living-room. The sofa was empty. She looked anxiously round for her doll, then she saw her. Nadine was sitting on the piano bench, a sheet of music on her lap.

overheard about the de Béards which troubled her. She thought
of her family, her grandparents in America and Tante Aimée
and Oncle Nigel Spencer in England, and again she thought of
Tante Hélène and Oncle Paul, and she could not believe it.

Mme Abbot and Mrs. Spencer were sisters and had been close
since childhood. Although one had married an American and
the other an Englishman, the bond of affection was further
strengthened by the very real friendship which existed between
their two husbands. In spite of having occasionally had a disturbing glimpse into other families, Mélanie carried within her
heart the unfounded assurance that all marriages were happy and
all families intimately bound by love and understanding.
Divorce was a word she had heard, but she thought it belonged
to another, a foreign language. It could not belong to her own,
but must have stumbled into it, as a Latin word will accidentally
slip into a French sentence.

So when she overheard someone say that the de Béards each
had been married before and that Françoise's much older
brother, Norbert, was Oncle Paul's son and not Tante Hélène's,
Mélanie dismissed this terrible thought as the kind of dark
folklore peasants were fond of recounting—something dim,
incomplete and far away, from the days when the Gauls first
settled France. But whenever Norbert called Mme de Béard
"*chère* Hélène" instead of "Maman," an unspecified nerve
quivered within Mélanie, and she wished he had not said it.
Desperately needing to have her mind put at rest, she finally
asked her mother if the words she had heard were true. Mme
Abbot looked at her daughter a second, then turned her head
away. Mélanie could see that her mother, too, wished to brush
the thought aside. She hastily tried to take her question back by
saying, "It doesn't matter, Maman."

Her mother answered slowly, "No, it does not matter. It was very long ago."

Mélanie felt certain of this, certain that it had taken place in the long ago before the Celts had invaded Brittany.

"Norbert's mother died," Mme Abbot continued, "and your Tante Hélène was very unhappy with the man she had first married. But now she is very happy with Oncle Paul."

Mélanie wished her mother had not said so much.

"Yes, I know," she replied, and she walked out of her mother's room into the nursery. She wanted to go where she could toss from her mind and, if possible, remove from reality, these two unknown people who had prevented Tante Hélène and Oncle Paul from always having been a pair, eternally inseparable, and married in the warm, loving, for ever sense.

For a long time afterwards she had stared at Mme de Béard, and then at her husband, to see if a look on their faces or a gesture might betray a past when they had not been together and someone else walked beside them. But when nothing in their voice or manner gave any hint of another life, Mélanie's fears fell away. And, once again, she became convinced that the de Béards had always been happily married to each other.

Norbert, who worked in a bank in Paris, was a worldly young man who went out socially a good deal; and Mélanie finally accepted his "*chère* Hélène" as something highly sophisticated, clever and tender, and she thought it was sweet and funny of him to use this endearment. So, she quietly made up her mind that when she grew up and became, in her turn, sophisticated and worldly, she would address her mother "*chère* Christine."

Mélanie was in a state of unparalleled ecstasy, for Easter meant a
reunion with her English cousins, the Spencers, and this year it
would take place in Brittany. The two families took turns
visiting each other, and since the Abbots had gone to England the
previous spring, it was the Spencers' turn to come to France.
Mme Abbot had told her children that they would not be going
to *Le Roc*, as it was not worth while to open the house for so
short a time, and that they would stay at the Grand Hotel instead.
This news was almost too much for Mélanie to take with calm
and serenity. If there was one place which to her was the acme
of glamour and excitement, it was the Grand Hotel in Kerouan.
High and terraced it stood on a grassy slope overlooking the
white oval of the casino, and the beach and sea beyond. The
main floor was a maze of living-rooms and halls, each shielding
heavily upholstered love seats behind potted palms. As long as
a child remained uncaught, it was magnificently suited to games
of hide-and-seek. With all the family gathered together, there
were bound to be outdoor pleasures, too, such as picnics and
surprises, rides in the car and teas in funny inns.

There was still one whole long week to go before the holiday
was officially begun, but Mélanie, Luc and Toinon could talk of
nothing else. Claude was not making much sense, because he got
Easter and the summer holiday mixed up in his mind, and he
was convinced that all their Paris friends would be in Brittany
also, which was nonsense. But he, too, was excited.

The older children were tutored every morning as usual, and
it became harder and harder for them to concentrate on their
studies. Mélanie tried to memorize the irregular verbs and the
names of the Merovingian kings, but she got so mixed up and
turned round, that she thought she never would get to the end
of them.

When the day of departure finally came, it was like no other day on earth. Beds were stripped of their linen, cupboards appeared strangely uncluttered, trunks lining the corridor were hurriedly jammed shut with a bang. Grown-ups were behaving like figures in a cuckoo clock; as soon as one left the room, another burst in. The telephone was in constant use. The children ran excitedly from one end of the flat to the other to keep abreast of all the activities, only to be chased to the opposite end again when an exasperated adult voice wailed, "Children, can't you stay out of the way!"

The cook was wrapping cheese and hard-boiled eggs in paper. At intervals, she would stop to wipe her eyes with her apron and mutter to herself: "The house won't be the same. It just won't be the same." Claude started to cry because he wanted to go to the lavatory, but there was no one there to fetch him the pot. When Mélanie darted off to search for it, she was told by Jeanne, the new maid, that it had probably been packed and not to bother her. Mélanie returned to the bathroom to find Luc trying to heave his brother on to the water-closet seat. She gave him a hand, but although they managed to get Claude to stand up, the joint effort was only partly successful, and their failure was dismally apparent on the tiled floor. The three of them set off in search of Toinon, more for consolation than out of concern. They found her squatting on the living-room floor, tightly clutching Bonhomme, her teddy bear. They sat down in silence, the four of them forming a guilty ring around the bear. They felt tense and useless. There was not much to say. At last, from their mother came the happy call, "*Les enfants, vite, en auto!*"

They scattered in four directions to pick up their favourite toys. Claude found the small boat without which he could not take a bath. Toinon held firmly to her teddy bear, and after some searching Luc unearthed his lorry. Mélanie knew exactly where she had left her doll. She went to the nursery and lifted her up from her carriage. Just as the four children reached the pavement and were about to climb into the car, Brigitte rushed out and announced, to the enlightenment of all passers-by: "They haven't been to the lavatory!" They meekly endured this humiliation and walked back into the building. On their return, Mme Abbot got in the car and Claude slid in beside her. Joël pulled down the jump seats, and the three eldest sat down. Brigitte, carrying coats and hats, got in front with the chauffeur. There was a long wait, and finally M. Abbot appeared and squeezed himself into the back seat. Mme Babette, Jeanne, and the concierge stood on the pavement. They waved and shouted, "*Bon voyage!* Have a good drive! We'll miss you!"

Joël let in the clutch. Mme Abbot let out an agonized cry: "*Le canari!*"

Everyone repeated after her, "*Le canari, le canari!*" The maid rushed into the build- ing. She returned, holding a gold-plated cage. Pip V was singing undisturbed. The cage was placed between Joël and Brigitte. There was a communal sigh of relief. The chauffeur let in the clutch once more. Happily waving, they were off!

Once on the country roads beyond the outskirts of Paris, Mélanie leant back and relaxed; the holiday had now really begun. She looked out of the window as the telephone poles shot past, their wires beaded with birds. She loved to see farm buildings held together by a stone courtyard. There was always a dog to bark at a passing car and one or more cackling hens venturing dangerously near the roadside. Children with dirty faces, in aprons or short dresses, scuttled busily about. The bent figures of men and women moved slowly through the furrowed fields. Every farm, Mélanie concluded, had an old man, short and bow-legged, leaning on a stick.

The roads were lined with trees planted at regular intervals, though the genus of the trees varied from province to province. There were many villages to drive through, each with a cobbled square, where Joël had to slow down and honk his horn. Old women in black crossed there on their way to market; old men sat on benches, dozing or reading newspapers, a handkerchief shielding their heads from the sun; dogs and cats took strolls; and children playing games sometimes darted in front of the car to drink at the public fountain. The danger averted, the car would pick up speed again, only to slow down anew at the next village. There were sudden curves, too, to be made around a wooden crucifix or a bronze statue of a boy in the uniform of the First World War.

As the sun-tipped poplars lining the road heralded their entrance into Normandy, the chauffeur looked back through the mirror and announced: "We're approaching Torreville, Monsieur."

M. Abbot turned to his wife and repeated, "We're approaching Torreville."

The children let out a squeal of delight. Joël's statement was the opening line to a familiar ritual. Every year at about the same spot, Joël would remind M. Abbot of the proximity of Torreville, and every year the same conversation and panto-mime followed. The children would glance slyly at the chauffeur through the mirror, and he would wink at them; then Mme

Abbot would turn to her husband and ask if they would not make more speed by stopping in a field further on and having a picnic lunch. M. Abbot would inquire if there was any wine in the picnic basket, and when he was told that they had only brought lemonade for the children, he would exchange a look with the chauffeur. The latter would grin back and say, quite casually, "Monsieur remembers that excellent Pauillac, 1920?"

Mélanie's father would then burst out laughing. The children, unable to keep silent another moment, would chime in, "And the cheese, Papa?"

The chauffeur would state, "The best in the country."

Brigitte then turned a pleading look towards Mme Abbot who answered it with a resigned shrug of the shoulder.

A child would exclaim, "*C'est décidé. On va chez Mme Chanat!*"

Everyone laughed and M. Abbot said, "All right, Joël, we'll stop in Torreville."

Torreville meant but one thing to the discerning traveller: the small, unpretentious inn where M. and Mme Chanat served the best cheese in the county and an unforgettable *paté maison*. In addition, the Chanats kept an excellently stocked wine cellar, so that for M. Abbot and the chauffeur this was not a place to be lightly by-passed.

In the Chanats' gravelled courtyard they were met by a barking collie and a flock of agitated geese. A wooden door creaked open and Mme Chanat, in a cotton dress and apron, appeared at the top of the outside stairs, which led to the dining-room on the second floor. On recognizing her visitors, she threw her arms in the air. "*Quelle surprise!*" she exclaimed.

She hastily pulled back the loose strands of hair that fell over her ears, wiped her hands vigorously against her apron, and rushed down to shake hands with the entire Abbot clan, all the while calling, "Auguste, Auguste! *Viens donc!*"

Her husband, in a yellowing white apron, soon came scurrying down, his arms extended, and echoing his wife's words. "*Quelle surprise!*"

With Mme Chanat in the lead, they all clambered up the wooden stairs and walked into a clean, sunlit room, where wooden tables were covered with red and white checked cloths. Two tables were pulled together, and the Abbot family sat down. The chauffeur discreetly ate alone in a small adjoining room. As both Chanats stood leaning expectantly against the table, M. Abbot pushed aside the handwritten menu and asked, "What do you recommend today?"

The couple smiled, nodded to each other, and Mme Chanat shrieked almost hysterically, "I know, I know! Leave it to me!" She nudged her husband reassuringly and both suddenly vanished into the kitchen. First came a huge French bread, then a mound of homemade butter, followed by the tensely awaited *paté*. It tasted like no other *paté* in the world and literally melted in the mouth. As the children kept dipping their knives into the central dish, Mme Abbot chided them, "Enough, enough, children. The meal has not yet started."

And sure enough, for Mme Chanat brought in a steaming dish of beef stew, cooked in wine. M. Chanat walked in behind her to discuss the wine list. After a long and sober discussion, a choice was made. M. Chanat stood anxious and silent while M. Abbot put the wine-filled glass to his lips. Mélanie watched her father tilt back his chair and utter a sensuous, satisfied, "Ah!" as M. Chanat nodded agreement, then she resumed her lunch.

After the steaming plate of asparagus and the bowl of green salad, M. Chanat brought in a huge tray with a selection of cheeses. Just as M. Abbot was about to cut into one with his knife, the kitchen door flew open and the innkeeper rushed in with a note from the chauffeur which read: "With all due respect to Monsieur, I have tried the Clos de Bèze, 1919, with the cheese. Excellent."

M. Abbot studied the note for several seconds. Then, handing it to M. Chanat, he said, "We'll have the same."

The children were allowed a sip of the Burgundy before being excused to run around the farm, while the others had their liqueur. When goodbyes and handshakes had been exchanged all round, with promises of a prompt return, the family settled heavily into the car. After a meal of this magnitude, no self-respecting person was expected to talk for a good half-hour or more. Eventually, the silence was broken by Joël who could hardly contain himself. "What did Monsieur think of the Clos de Bèze?"

This was the start of a solemn exchange of comparisons and reminiscences, a careful weighing of wines tasted or yet untried, which, although Greek to the children, delighted them. As they approached Kerouan, however, the conversation took a more general turn, and small fingers began pointing through the windows at familiar landmarks.

"Look, there's that old man again and his wagon!"

"Remember that funny tree?"

"This road hasn't changed at all!"

And anticipation made the children wriggle in their seats. Soon, Kerouan itself rumbled beneath the wheels. The public square, with its Gothic church as the focal point, the stone sea-wall, the harbour with its fishing boats gently knocking at anchor, and in the distance, the scattered islands, each with its history and legend. The main street stretching parallel to the sea, and, at last, the Grand Hotel!

But to everyone's dismay, no light shone its welcome. The Grand Hotel was closed, with every one of its shutters drawn tight. The children were speechless with distress. The chauffeur got out of the car, looked around, then honked the horn several times. A man shouted from across the street, and there on the terrace of the hotel's annexe stood the proprietor. He was waving to them and from behind him, lights quivered at every window.

"*Ici! Ici!*" he shouted.

There was a helter-skelter dash across the street, and through shouts and greetings, the explanation took shape. The Grand Hotel was closed until the opening of the summer season, but the annexe was kept open all winter, and the proprietor felt certain that they would be just as comfortable, if not more so. The annexe was smaller, warmer, more intimate. The Abbots would have a whole floor to themselves, and the Spencers the one below.

The children raced around, peeking into every room, while trunks and suitcases were hoisted upstairs.

"I want to sleep here," Toinon announced, as she sat down on one of the two brass beds. From the tone of her sister's voice, Mélanie sensed that this was a point not to be argued, so she sat down to acquaint herself with the bed that had been scorned. While Brigitte unpacked and arranged cupboards, the children leant out of the windows to comment on the passers-by and whatever changes the street had undergone since they had seen it the summer before.

An early supper was brought up for Claude, who could hardly keep his eyes open, but the other children were told to come with their parents to the dining-room. A fire gleamed in the fireplace. Candles flickered on the tables. After seating themselves, the Abbots looked around at the other diners. Two middle-aged Englishmen, with spats on their shoes and flowers in their button-holes, sat by a window. At another table sat two elderly ladies in tweeds and a gentleman in plus-fours. Obviously, English, too. The table farthest away was occupied by a soft-spoken French couple. The young Abbots noted with chagrin that there was no sign of other children staying at the annexe, but the thought of their English cousins soon to arrive made this disappointment easier to bear.

The next day M. and Mme Abbot drove to the station to meet

the afternoon train and the Spencers, leaving their offspring to wait impatiently on the hotel terrace. When the car at last returned, the four Abbots ran down to meet their cousins with shouts of delight. Unaccustomed as the two Spencer children were to affectionate demonstrations, they nevertheless yearly submitted to the Gallic embraces of their less restrained kinsmen. In spite of dissimilar environments and of the inherent difference between an Anglo-Saxon and a Latin upbringing, the cousins were extremely fond of each other. The two Spencers were thin and blond; the four Abbots, sturdy and dark, but the difference in colouring, language and education proved no barrier between cousins. If four of them spoke no more than a dozen words of English, Peter and Anne had a better command of French, and they had no trouble understanding one another.

M. and Mme Spencer went inside to unpack, but the six children, with Brigitte and the Spencers' English nanny, set off for their first walk to the beach. It was a beautiful, clear, cool April day, carrying within itself hints and hopes of an early spring. The beach was empty. Held between two walls of rock, its crescent shape was distended to an almost full moon by the lowness of the tide. A foreigner on holiday occasionally passed by on the promenade, briskly taking his constitutional. The children built a castle out of the wet sand. Claude hovered round it, a menace to its longevity, and was unceremoniously shooed away. With his shovel and pail he made a mound of his own, as close by as he was allowed to get. Contentedly, the cousins carried sand in their shoes and mud on their socks; but the breeze, blowing a cool current in the bay, soon chased them back to the hotel, to hot baths and early supper.

of the first two days had died down, the Abbot children, having taken their evening baths, walked down to the floor below. They knocked on their cousins' door. Peter opened it, and Mélanie announced, "We've come to kiss you goodnight."

The English cousins stood in their pyjamas with a look of horror on their faces.

"Oh no," Anne cried out, "you needn't bother!"

"But we want to," Luc insisted.

"Kiss everybody!" Claude sang out.

"You must be mad." Peter, who, like Luc, was almost seven, sounded like an old man.

"You're our cousins," Toinon pointed out the undeniable fact and sat down on a bed to wait.

Mélanie explained, with a note of frustration in her voice, "We always kiss our family goodnight."

"In England, it's not done," Peter said firmly. Then he added somewhat affectedly, "Disgusting!"

"Is that so!" Luc whirled round.

"Yes, it's so," Peter chimed back.

Claude, as always unaware of danger, snuggled up to Anne and cooed, "Kiss Claude. Kiss Claude goodnight."

But his cousin gently pushed him away with the words, "Silly baby!"

Claude rushed over to his elder sister, his feelings hurt. She hugged him, but she was beginning to feel uncomfortable.

"Let's go upstairs," she said, pulling Claude towards the door.

Luc opened the wedge a second time, his voice unsteady. "We've only come to say goodnight. In France, people are polite."

"Ha," Peter sniffed, "In France, people are snivelling idiots!"

That was too much for the Abbots.

"Why do you come here then for your holidays?" Mélanie was furious. She felt herself about to turn into a mean person and not a cousin at all.

"Because," Peter said with exaggerated patience, "our parents drag us over here to visit you, you drooling French cousins!"

"Peter!" Anne interjected feebly.

"Well, we have plenty of other cousins," Mélanie heard herself say. "We don't need you."

"And we have some, decent, well-behaved cousins of our own!" Peter asserted.

"Then take the boat back and go and see them." Mélanie saw that Luc was turning into a mean person, too.

"Let's go," she said, and still holding on to Claude, she walked out into the hall.

"Goodbye," Luc shouted and walked out after her.

Toinon said a feeble, "Goodnight, Anne," and rose from the bed. Anne and she were the same age and obviously wished they had had nothing to do with this scene.

"Well," Luc said as they all traipsed up to their rooms, "fine cousins, they are!"

"All the English are stuffy," Mélanie had heard someone say this, but she was not very happy saying it herself.

"Anne is a nice cousin," Toinon ventured despondently as she climbed into bed.

"Well, she's stuffy, too," Luc said.

They all got into bed, the door between the boys' room and the girls' room remained ajar. Mélanie lay awake thinking and watching the cars below shoot square shadows on the ceiling.

"Luc, do you suppose they will ever kiss us goodnight?"

There was a short pause. Then, sounding strangely loud and final in the darkness, his answer came.

"*Ces Anglais? Jamais!*"

Luc and Mélanie were walking down the main street of Kerouan
as fast as they could go, on either side of their father. Although
they considered it a treat to go out with him, no matter what the
pretext, it did mean that they had to hop or skip the whole way
in order to keep up with the stride of his long legs. They were
now all three headed for the pharmacy to pick up a prescription
for Toinon, who was in bed with a slight cold. As they rushed
past the *confiserie*, Mélanie had a fleeting glimpse of a *"chien de
crise"* in the window. A picture flashed through her mind of her
grandparents, their faces flushed with fever, and an old anxiety
sank into her heart. She felt herself becoming a very brave person
and boldly asked, "Papa, *Grand-père et Grand'mère*, are they in
great pain?"

M. Abbot came to an abrupt halt, looked strangely at his
daughter and asked, "What do you mean?"

She hesitated before continuing. "I mean," she stammered,
"does the Depression hurt?"

"Hurt!" M. Abbot exclaimed. "What are you trying to
say?"

"She means," Luc broke in, "does the doctor have to come
and give them pills and things?"

Mélanie was startled; so Luc had been wondering about it, too.
Their father let out an amused chuckle. Taking them each by
the hand, he started up the street again.

"We'll pick up the prescription," he said, "then I'll tell you
about the Depression."

On their way back from the chemist, M. Abbot walked more
slowly.

"Well now, about the Depression . . ." he began. "Men work
hard to make money so that their wives and children can have a
nice house to live in, pretty clothes to wear and enough food to

eat. What money they have left over, they put in a bank. These savings, as this money is called, are an insurance against the future. When a child is of age to go to school or university, a father draws on this money to pay the tuition; or a man may use these savings to retire and stay at home with his family. Well, money is a complex business which goes under the name of economics. When an economy is unstable, banks may go bankrupt; that is, the money isn't there any more. This is what has happened in America. Lots and lots of people have lost their money."

"*Grand-père et Grand'mère*, too?" Luc asked.

"Yes," their father answered. "They, too, have lost some money."

"Are they starving?" Mélanie queried. She had a fleeting vision of her beloved grandparents, a tin bowl in their hands, begging in the streets.

"No," M. Abbot was smiling. "They're all right. They are still living in the big house and they have enough to eat."

"Are they sad?" Luc asked.

"I don't believe so. If they are, it is because so many people are so much less fortunate than they are."

Mélanie burst out laughing. In fact, she laughed so hard that she could not stop. And then Luc started to laugh. They could hardly go on walking but had to stop and hold their stomachs. Their father shook them. "What's the matter with you two?"

And the more he shook them, the more they laughed. Mélanie thought of her grandparents without a fever or a single pimple to mar their kind, lined faces, and she felt dizzy and light, as if her interior box had overturned and scattered its contents on the pavement.

All of a sudden Luc stopped laughing and announced, "I want a *chien de crise*, Papa."

"I do, too!" Mélanie tittered.

"Whatever for?" and the bewilderment in M. Abbot's voice started them off giggling again.

"I just want one," Luc repeated.

"Me, too!"

There was a long silence before M. Abbot spoke again. "Show me one."

Mélanie gave his sleeve a tug and led him to the *confiserie*. Peering at them from the window was a small, thin grey poodle.

"What do you want one of those for?"

Obviously M. Abbot did not understand. Mélanie did not quite know how to tell him. "For *Grand'mère* and *Grand-père*," she ventured timidly.

M. Abbot stared at his children a minute, then, finally, he said: "Ah . . ."

Their father always said "Ah" when he understood. They went into the store.

"How much are these silly things?" he inquired of the girl behind the counter. When he was told the price, he peered down at his children, a serious look on his face. "They're expensive."

Mélanie and Luc looked at one another. Mélanie felt a great bond with her brother at that moment, for he, too, had borne the same uneasiness in silence. Their secrets were, perhaps, not so dissimilar after all. They both glanced up at their father, not knowing what to say. M. Abbot looked searchingly into their faces. "Would you share one?"

"Oh yes, yes, we would!" brother and sister chorused.

They heard their father's voice over the counter. "One, please. Don't wrap it."

Luc carried it home.

"We'll call him Crise," Mélanie whispered.

"Crisie," Luc corrected.

"Yes, Crisie," Mélanie echoed.

And they hurried back to the hotel to show the dog to Toinon.

by the sound of sobs on the landing. She opened her bedroom door. Brigitte and Nanny were bent over Anne, who was saying something incoherent about a cat. It seemed she had found a cat, but he had escaped from her arms. Mélanie turned at the sound of footsteps and there, mounting the stairs, was Toinon, a shabby orange cat clutched under her arm. When Toinon spotted her weeping cousin, she, too, burst into tears.

Disgusted, Mélanie went back into her room. She picked up *Les Malheurs de Sophie*, which she had been reading, but she could no longer keep her mind on it. Why do people make such a fuss over animals? she wondered. She, herself, rather fancied peacocks and zebras, but pets she could see no use for. Mme Abbot loved the canary and she also had a strange weakness for dogs. If M. Abbot had not put his foot down periodically, their Paris flat would long ago have been turned into a kennel. Claude, Toinon and Luc always wanted to keep turtles, mice and snails, but Mélanie did not like the mess animals made, nor had she ever enjoyed the feeling of a moist snout against her bare legs.

She went back to the doorway to look. The two girls were sobbing loudly while Brigitte and Nanny, one in French and one in English, were explaining how little girls could not keep every stray cat they found, how cats preferred the outdoors to living in flats, whether in Paris or London, that no doubt the cat had a perfectly good home of its own somewhere, and so on and so on. What a fuss! Mélanie thought. Anne's face was peaked, her eyes were flushed and red. Toinon, still clutching the animal under discussion, looked the picture of despair. Mélanie's legs suddenly felt weak, and, inexplicably moved by compassion, she asked, "Why can't they keep the cat until we leave?"

Both women turned, an astonished scowl on their faces. Mélanie went back into her room and slammed the door.

The girls were finally permitted to keep the cat, with the understanding that M. Bric-à-Brac would be notified. The town crier made his announcements once a week. He brought news of births and deaths, of items lost or found, and, if need be, of wars and assassinations. The remainder of the week he sat in a canvas chair in front of his miscellaneous second-hand shop. Behind, on the window pane, one could read the letters: "bric-à-brac." By this name he came to be known by most of the children of Kerouan, although in the adult world he answered to the name of Père Meulin.

So, that week, he took his accustomed stand in front of the now-empty Grand Hotel. His massive drum hung from a strap around his neck and, before speaking, he beat a deafening roll on it, while his thin grey hair stirred gently in the breeze. He wore no tie, and his baggy trousers were loosely held to his heavy frame by unmatched braces. The Spencers and Abbots stood on the terrace of the annexe opposite, as he announced the tides for the coming week, the death of Mme Ramier, widow and lace worker, the hour of the funeral, and a special sale at his own shop the next day. At last he came to the cat. In loud tones he proclaimed that Mlle Anne Spencer and Mlle Antoinette Abbot had found a starved cat of orange hue, on April the 9th, near the Rue . . . , etc. Anne and Toinon enjoyed hearing their names bellowed with such solemnity, but no one claimed the cat that day or thereafter. His origins were to be for ever clouded in mystery.

The cat took to his new mistresses with dignified detachment. Mélanie was careful always to be busy when he meowed to go out or to be fed. She tried hard for the remainder of the holiday to pretend that the cat did not exist and that Toinon and Anne were no less normal than before. But it was impossible completely to ignore their frightful and inane enslavement to this haughty and oddly expressionless stray. They locked him in a bedroom when they went to the beach and worried lest he should get out. They worried about him while they ate and took turns sneaking out of bed at night, to see that he was not too lonely in the bathroom.

When they left Kerouan, the cat was entrusted to the hotel owner who assured the young ladies that the stray could not be in better hands. But Mélanie experienced a fiendish pleasure at a ghastly vision which passed briefly before her eyes. She pictured the proprietor waiting for the car to disappear round the bend, then, patting the cat's rump, sending him out into the street again.

But when the Abbots had seen the Spencers off on the train and were speeding back towards Paris, Mélanie felt a warm glow in her heart. It had been a lovely, relaxed holiday. The cousins had built innumerable castles in the sand and collected enough shells to sink the night boat from Calais to Dover. They had fished among the rocks and almost pulled each other's legs off, imitating wheelbarrows. Uncle Nigel had had his face licked by a cow on a picnic, and M. Abbot had almost driven them into a sand bar when he hired a boat to sail them to the outlying islands. And now the Abbot children were returning to the city with some delicious new words, such as "ripping," "posh," and "super," while the young Spencers were exporting *"épatant," "rigolo,"* and *"formidable."*

ALTHOUGH SHE WAS ABOUT TO CELEBRATE her ninth birthday, Mélanie felt sad. Her father had gone on a business trip to the Balkans, and for the first time he would not be there to see her safely embarked on a new year. She wandered about the flat, restless and unreconciled, until the ring of the doorbell told her that Françoise had arrived and lunch would soon be served. Mélanie almost stumbled as she ran to meet her friend. But in the living-room both girls held hands, self-consciously waiting in their best velvet dresses for something to happen. It was with some relief that they heard Mme Abbot call out: "Luc, go and fetch Brigitte. And Toinon, tell them in the kitchen that we're ready."

When Mme Abbot opened the double doors to the dining-room Brigitte, Mme Babette, Jeanne and Joël, holding a small bouquet of violets, were lined up against the highboy. As everyone sang, "Happy Birthday!" in doubtful unison, Mélanie gazed spellbound at the red and white cake aglow with nine candles, in the centre of the table. Her heart was beating so fast that she was afraid to speak. Finally, she glanced round the room and saw her doll propped up in a chair, looking prettier than ever before in a pink dress, with shoes and socks to match.

"Oh, Maman," she exclaimed, "how pretty she looks!"

Joël broke into an amused chuckle and handed her the nosegay. "This is a small remembrance from us all," he said.

Mélanie threw her arms about his neck. When she had kissed the other servants, Mme Babette led the procession back into the pantry. Mélanie returned to the contemplation of her cake. She closed her eyes to make a wish. She wished that her father might always be present on her birthdays; then she blew very long and hard, and finally all the candles went out. But there were other things on the table: a book by the Countess de Ségur from her brothers and sister, and a box of chocolates from Françoise. After rising to thank each one, Mélanie went back to her chair, for she had noticed a large and awkward package. It disclosed a miniature piano. Attached to it was a note which read: "For Nadine's piano lesson—signed, Nicholas." The piano

was a bright red and just the right size for her doll. This was a better birthday than anything she could have dreamed. But that was not all. On her plate was a telegram addressed to Mlle Abbot. She looked inquiringly at her mother.

"It's for you. Open it."

Mélanie took a knife and cut around the blue paper with great care. It was the first telegram she had ever received, and she had to look at it awhile before she could concentrate enough to read it.

"IT HAS BEEN LOVELY HAVING YOU FOR MY ELDEST DAUGHTER THE PAST EIGHT YEARS STOP AM LOOKING FORWARD TO BEING YOUR PROUD FATHER FOR MANY YEARS TO COME STOP BRINGING SURPRISE STOP PAPA."

It was too much! Mélanie clasped her doll tightly against her chest and repeated absurdly: "It's from Papa! It's from Papa!"

She came back down to earth when her mother pressed the button under the table and said, "Well, now we can start lunch."

In deference to the occasion, there were to be no naps that day; instead Mme Abbot would take the children calling, and Nadine could come along to show off her new dress. As they drove off in the car, Mélanie allowed Françoise to hold the doll on her knee, but when they started to climb the stairs to Grande-Tante's apartment, she reclaimed her.

Mme Abbot's aunt was a spry ninety-three. She was small, white-haired, pale-skinned and blue-veined. She still dressed in the style of the Third Empire, only now she always wore black. She had on a black taffeta dress with a button-tight bodice, topped by a velvet ruching. Her skirt was wide and came to meet the heel of her black laced bootees. Her bonnet—it was not really a hat—was made of taffeta ribbon and tied under her chin. Ever since Mélanie had known her, she had been living on an inadequate pension. Her apartment, cluttered with furniture and bibelots, was small and airless. Nevertheless, it was elegant. On the marble fireplace stood a yellowed photograph, framed in gold. It was a portrait of the Empress Eugénie, sitting on a garden bench; a pretty round-faced young girl sat smiling on the grass in front of her. It was Grande-Tante. A huge canopied bed dominated the old lady's bedroom next door. On the bedside table a round frame edged the handsome, smiling face of Grand-Oncle, as he had been as a young man, an officer on Louis Napoleon's staff, in love and wooing the little round-faced girl in the other picture.

Grande-Tante was always delighted to receive callers. After properly admiring the quality and cut of Nadine's new costume, she went to the kitchen in search of some orangeade.

As a child will toy with a single thought or notion until he has driven all about him to the extreme edge of lunacy, so, too, Grande-Tante nursed an obsession from which no amount of persuasion could divert her mind or deter her will. She never failed to bring up the subject each time the children visited her, and the ritualistic aspect of this repetition only added to their delight. When the "*bonne*" had carried in the pitcher of orangeade and Grande-Tante had returned to her chair, she plunged into the subject immediately. She was obsessed with a desire to fly. She wanted to go for a drive, as she called it, in an aeroplane. The poor condition of her heart, however, precluded any such flights, save in the realm of fancy. For years her nephews and nieces had done their best to dissuade her, but she would relinquish neither the idea, the hope, nor the contemplation of it. In a final desperate effort at assuagement, her kinsmen made her a promise. When she reached her hundredth birthday, they would celebrate by hiring a plane to fly her over Paris. Her unfading blue eyes merely twinkled more mischievously; all she had to do was to wait and check off the years on the calendar.

Why Grande-Tante should so want to fly was a mystery to

the young Abbots. She, herself, explained it this way: "When I was a girl, no one dreamed that within his lifetime people would actually travel in the air. But I saw the first balloon go up, the first aeroplane and the first dirigible. So it is that I have seen a whole new world open up. I want to get a taste of it before I die."

Mélanie thought it was wonderfully daring and intrepid of her great-aunt to wish to experience this new world and wondered why she, herself, had never questioned it and felt, as yet, no need to be a part of it.

Sitting in a huge arm-chair, her feet poised on a footstool, Grande-Tante looked like an old-fashioned doll; the kind one might come upon in an antique shop, unaccountably fall in love with and pay for at once in order to whisk her home without delay. She fitted perfectly the romantic conception of an old lady. She wore no make-up. Her face was finely wrinkled and translucent. The scent of lavender emanated from her clothes as she sat, gay, sedate, decided and childlike.

"Did you really dance with Napoleon?" Toinon asked, leaning against the old lady's chair.

"But of course I did," Grande-Tante replied, with the same zestful tone she always used when asked the question.

"Show us how it happened!" Toinon's face glowed with anticipation.

"But I've told you before," Grande-Tante protested though her voice was soft and there was no denial in it.

"Oh, tell us again!" the children chorused. They hurried to the sofa to sit in a tight, expectant row, as though taking their places in a theatre.

"Well," Grande-Tante began, then she hesitated to turn a questioning look on Françoise, but the girl had squeezed herself between Luc and Mélanie and she, too, was waiting.

"Well, I was only eighteen. I had not yet met Grand-Oncle. There was to be a ball at the palace, and my mother had received an invitation for us both. It was my first big ball and, oh, I was so excited! I danced quite well in those days, if I may say so," and there was a coquettish glint in her eye, "for I had been well instructed by M. du Mans. But dancing at a ball and with strangers was new to me. Well, we walked into the throne room and were introduced, one by one, by the chamberlain. His Imperial Highness was in uniform with medals, lots of them, blazing on his chest, and he looked so majestic and handsome with his black goatee. The Empress sat on a red velvet chair, in a white satin dress. She was young and so beautiful. They looked just as an Emperor and Empress should look. Ah, France could be proud of herself in those days!"

This was not the impression Mélanie had gleaned from her history book, which was written by an educator of the Third Republic; but Grande-Tante had witnessed grandeurs unsurpassed by anything Mélanie had ever seen, and she did not find it difficult to believe that France had been proud more than once.

"And what did you wear, Grande-Tante?" Toinon interrupted. The Abbots knew exactly what she had worn, but they loved hearing every detail anew.

"I wore a dress," the old lady continued, smiling at herself as though visualizing it for the first time, "made of brocade. It had a beige, no, an almost pink background with tiny pale green leaves woven in it." She rose from her chair. She had now quite forgotten her listeners and was back at the palace—a proud, shy girl at court for the first time. "The neck was like this," and with her fingers she drew a crescent below her shoulders. "It had a little bustle," and she turned her back to her audience that they might picture the bustle. And, sure enough, the children saw it clearly: the small slim figure, the pink and green bustle, and the young girl standing erect, eyes down, about to curtsey before her Emperor. "I wore a pendant that my father had left me. It was a pink cameo held up by a thin gold chain. When my name was called, I curtsied like this," and the nonagenarian made a flawless curtsey before the spellbound children. They were no longer mere onlookers or intruders into the past but had now become Eugénie and Louis Napoleon themselves, gazing at the lovely young girl. "When everyone had been presented, we lined up on both sides of the room to make an aisle for their Highnesses. The Emperor held the Empress's arm, and they slowly marched down between us. I could have reached out and touched her gown with my hand."

There was a breathless "Oh!" from Françoise, but Grande-Tante did not appear to hear it.

"The Emperor opened the ball by dancing with the Empress, and we all stood in a circle to watch them. How gracefully they danced together!" She stopped, seemingly to savour the inner images of her mind.

"Go on. Go on!" Toinon urged.

"Well, I was standing next to my mother when the Emperor came towards us. When he asked her if I might dance with him, I could hardly believe my ears. The orchestra was playing a waltz. The Emperor took me by the waist, and, before I had quite grasped what was happening, we were dancing!"

And in the middle of the cluttered living-room, the old lady was holding up her skirt with her left hand, while her right arm was raised high above her; she was dancing with Napoleon III. . . .

"He was so gallant! We were going around, one, two three . . . one, two three. Then he said, 'You dance extremely well, Mlle de la Vonne!'"

And Grande-Tante whirled about the room until the tune in her head came to a stop. The children clapped and clapped. For many years to come they would be firmly convinced that they had been at court on that memorable evening, hidden witnesses to Mlle de la Vonne's first ball.

When they had said their good-byes to Grande-Tante, leaving her slightly out of breath and only partially re-entrenched in the twentieth century, the Abbots went to call on Tante Berthe and Oncle Étienne, who were cousins of Mme Abbot.

Tante Berthe was the best person to visit at tea-time because she did her own baking and her pantry was always lined with tin boxes filled with biscuits, buns and chocolate cake. She liked to urge young visitors to eat a little more of this or that, or try a "*tarte aux fraises*" made just that day; and even when the children were so full that the only hunger remaining was one of the retina and not of the stomach, they ate on under her gentle, eager prodding. And whenever they left her flat, it was all they could do to stagger down the three flights of stairs and fall into the car.

But it was Oncle Étienne who, through no exertion of his own, had cast a spell on the young Abbots. He was short, with a magnificent head of black silken hair, and he sported a beard. Soft, clean and slightly scented it cascaded over his discreetly protruding paunch, covering his gold watch and chain. And when Mélanie kissed him, she liked to linger a moment with her cheek against his beard, her arms stiffly trying to encircle his convex waist.

Once, long ago, when she had pulled at his beard to see whether it hurt or would come off, he had warned her to be careful, or she would disturb the bird who made his nest in it. And later when, one after the other, the children had searched his beard in the hope of uncovering the nest, they had had to do it with such care that they never found it. Now, part of Mélanie's mind no longer believed that the beard had ever sheltered a bird, but in another part, hope lingered still.

After tea, while they sat around in the living-room listening to the grown-ups, the children kept very still, their eyes fixed on Oncle Étienne, in case the bird should unexpectedly fly out. But it did not, not even today on Mélanie's birthday, and Claude turned to look at his older sister with an expression which plainly asked for a re-affirmation of his faith. But Mélanie did not know how to answer it. She stared at her uncle quizzically and sharply, before shaking hands in parting, wondering whether a man with such gentle brown eyes could possibly tell a lie.

When they had returned to their flat, after driving Françoise home, Mélanie rushed into the nursery to give Nadine her first piano lesson. And if she had ever had a nicer birthday, she did not remember when that possibly could have been.

to Mme Abbot to say that her son was to be in a school play and
hoped that Luc and Mélanie might be able to come and see it.
Mme Abbot accepted the invitation and accompanied her two
eldest to the boarding school on the outskirts of Paris which
Amaury attended. Mélanie was delighted that Amaury had
wanted her to be there, but she was more excited still at the
prospect of seeing him act. It was to be a shortened French
version of *A Midsummer Night's Dream*.

In the school auditorium, which was a partly converted greenhouse, Mélanie and her brother sat erect and expectant in the
front row. As she stared at the greying and threadbare curtain
before her, she felt sure that all anyone could ever hope to see
or hear or know of the mysteries of life was about to be revealed
to her.

When the three taps of a stick backstage announced that the
play was about to begin, she almost stopped breathing. The curtains parted, and she let out a small, inarticulate cry. The gold and
white Greek palace was more regal and awesome than any castle
she had ever read about. Her initial disappointment at not seeing
Amaury on stage at the onset was soon forgotten in her complete
absorption in the cadences and movements of the players. She
had no past, no future. Her self-awareness was submerged by this
other, this peripheral living. The forest in the second act was more
mysterious and more splendid than any fairyland she had read
about. And when Amaury made his appearance as Oberon,
Mélanie had to put her hand to her mouth in order not to let
out a squeal of delight. He looked so frail and other-wordly that
she could not imagine him playing any other rôle but that of
the enchanted king of the forest.

The intervals proved merely an annoying suspension of the
dream, during which she had a hard time spotting her mother

in the crowd and a long wait at the outdoor water fountain. When the play came to an end she could not move and would have sat on, transfixed and contented, if Luc had not pulled at her sleeve and said, "Oh, come on, Mélanie! It's tea-time."

At the far end of the greenhouse, wives of the staff were serving tea and biscuits, while parents and students milled round. Mélanie searched in vain for her hero. When he finally arrived, make-up still visible here and there on his otherwise clean face, she held out her hand, and all her delight, admiration and awe were expressed in her short exclamation, "Oh, Amaury!"

He grinned as though she had crowned him king of the earth, and indeed she felt that she had. Together they went to the buffet table to claim their share of biscuits. Holding hands they walked away, unsteadily balancing their plates with the other.

"I want to show you the piano," he said.

They went out through the French doors, past the gravel courtyard and into the main building. At the end of a long corridor, Amaury pushed a door ajar with his foot. The walls of the room were lined with books. On top of the grand piano, sheets of music were piled high. Music stands stood around at jaunty angles. The two children put their plates down on a chair. Amaury sat down on the wooden piano bench and beckoned to Mélanie to sit beside him. His fingers moved lightly over the keys, then he struck a chord. He turned to smile at his listener and dreamily started to play a Chopin prélude. Mélanie's admiration for her young cavalier was now without bounds. Looking out through the wide windows at the formal garden beyond, she sat transported and enthralled. She was far away when Amaury stopped playing. He was the first to speak. "Mélanie . . . when I grow up, will you marry me?"

She looked deeply into his grave black eyes. They looked back at her, gentle and unblinking. At this moment she would have liked to be his forest queen for ever, but other and contradictory emotions assailed her. There was Nicholas, the father of Nadine. He, too, was a musician and a man of charm and unquestionable genius. Her feelings for him had deeper roots, strong, passionate tentacles that kept her heart a dedicated prisoner. Amaury was nearer her age, understanding and loyal, and the affection she had for him was pure and faithful, but she wondered if it did not lack the intensity necessary to assure eternal fidelity. She felt certain too, that while there was plenty of time before the issue came to a head, when it did, her parents would press Frank upon her. But there Mélanie would be firm. She would say no, with dignified finality, and then, leading Amaury, or perhaps Nicholas —it was a hard choice to make—by the hand, she would announce, "*Je suis fiancée.*"

Her parents would be so impressed by the sagacity of her selection that, although Frank was bound to weep bitter tears, the matter would be settled most satisfactorily.

"I'd like to," she answered with the utmost sincerity, "but I can't marry until I am seventeen, and then, of course, Maman and Papa will want me to marry Frank." She heaved a heavy sigh. "The whole thing will be a mess."

"Yes, I see . . ." Amaury's voice trailed softly off into the vastness of the room.

"But when I am seventeen," she went on absently, picturing herself tall and beautiful in a tulle dress, "I'll decide for myself."

Why she chose the age of seventeen for her betrothal date, she was not sure. She knew that she was not expected to become a lady, in the full-fledged sense of the word, until she was eighteen. Advancing the date by a year, she was perhaps shortening the time as much as she dared. There was a long pause as both children munched their biscuits.

"Maybe we could get engaged just the same," Amaury suggested.

"Maybe," Mélanie thought for a while. "Yes, that would be very nice."

They rose. Amaury gripped her hand firmly in his. "We're secretly engaged," he said.

They stood uncertain a moment, as though perhaps there should have been more to the ceremony, and they had forgotten something. But since nothing further seemed to be happening, no distant music rang in their ears, no mature revelation came to them, the room in no way altered its appearance, all was as before, they walked out hand in hand and made their way back to the greenhouse.

That evening Mélanie realized that she had become a new and beautiful person—a girl secretly engaged to Amaury.

NEITHER LANGUAGES NOR GOVERNESSES HAD been referred to for some time, as Brigitte quietly, almost unobtrusively, took over Nurse's duties. In the Luxembourg Gardens she sat reading near a grove of chestnut trees, a spot of her own choosing, on the opposite terrace from the one where Jacques, no doubt, still watched the recent film releases of M. l'Ingénieur. Here, a pleasant surprise awaited the Abbot children. René, who had once headed "the road," was now in charge of this section of the park. He seemed genuinely glad to see his old friends again and promptly introduced them to all the children under his command. Thanks to this unexpected stroke of fortune, the Abbots felt immediately at home in their new surroundings. When Mélanie and Luc told René how they had lost the road, he showed no surprise, for he was in a similar predicament. His stretch of land was threatened by a boy named Dujardin, who organized periodic raids, stealing bicycles, penknives, purses, anything he could lay his hands on. His henchmen called themselves "*les Jardiniers*," as a pun on their chief's name.

But as the days rolled by and the enemy kept out of sight, Mélanie who, unlike Damocles, was used to living under threat of peril, chased her hoop and took her doll for strolls, her mind at ease. With René in charge, she felt safe.

Several weeks passed peacefully before she had her first disturbing experience. She had been pushing her doll carriage and had just entered the grove of chestnut trees, when she became conscious that someone was watching her. She looked up and saw a few feet ahead of her a boy of about thirteen fixedly staring at her. Instinctively, she wheeled the carriage round and headed back towards the unshaded expanse of the terrace. Although she had given her observer but a quick, superficial glance, she had noticed the colourless brown of his wispy, untidy hair and the defects of his ill-fitting brown coat, which no longer buttoned across his chest and was too short in the sleeves. The boy had been staring at her while chewing on the end of a roll of liquorice, and she had noted with distaste the black sticky rim encircling his slightly too red lips. However, once back under the open sky, surrounded by children whose names she now knew, she soon forgot the boy.

A week later she saw him again. René and his friends were in the middle of a vast game of hide-and-seek, involving about twenty children. Mélanie had raced down the terrace stairs with the intention of hiding behind the boat renter's cart. Seeing that the old man was not in his accustomed place, but was pushing his cart round the pond in search of trade, she changed her plans and ran for shelter into one of the empty sentry-boxes which were used by the guards in bad weather. Each one had three walls and no door and was built to hold only one man. Mélanie

129

sat on the wooden seat and waited, certain that she would not be discovered for some time. She heard running footsteps outside, but since there were no warning calls, she ascribed them to some other group of children. Suddenly, the footsteps came to an abrupt halt and Mélanie found herself surrounded by half a dozen unknown boys. Faint with fright, she jumped to her feet and, leaning hard against the wall, faced her intruders.

"There she is," one of them stated flatly.

"We've got her," another grinned.

"We'd better hurry before he gets here," a third boy said.

Mélanie wondered if she were overhearing a conversation in a nightmare.

"Raise your skirt," the first boy ordered.

Automatically, her hands came down to shield herself.

"Do as we say, and hurry," he commanded again.

Mélanie did not move.

Another boy stuck his head in. "You know who we are? We're *les Jardiniers*, so no nonsense!"

She could see six faces, six grim and unyielding faces, gazing at her. As she remained motionless, the first boy placed one foot in the cabin and, reaching out, tugged at her skirt.

"No!" she cried, making a helpless gesture towards her clothes. A second boy stepped into the sentry-box, thrusting the first boy forward. Mélanie lost sight of the blue edge of sky, and, in the sudden darkness, she felt smothered by the heavy breathing of the boy leaning against her. She jerked her head aside and, there, coming up behind her assailants, she recognized the boy who had stared at her in the grove of chestnut trees. His lips were still edged with black, his thin hair was still uncombed. He moved with self-assurance as he tapped one of the boys on the shoulder. "*Allons!*"

The six boys turned to face him. He repeated, "*Allons! Allons, les gars!*" and with a raised movement of the shoulders, he signalled them to follow him. The first boy released his hold on Mélanie and stepped out of the cabin. In a moment they were gone. Mélanie took a deep breath, looked up at the vast expanse of sky, then straightening her clothes, she tore out of the sentry-box, and up the stairs, where she almost collided with René.

"Where have you been?" he asked, but before she could catch her breath, he continued, "They've stolen again! While **we** were off playing, they took Henri's scooter, Louise's pram, and I don't know what else. We've got to be more . . ."

Mélanie interrupted him. "René, I've seen Dujardin."

"*Non! C'est vrai?*"

"Yes. He rescued me. He eats liquorice."

"That's him! Come over here. . . ."

Mélanie allowed him to lead her by the stone balustrade, where a wooden crate served as his Commander's Seat. He pulled it out for her to sit on, while he crouched on the ground. "What happened?"

She gave him a brief account of what had taken place.

"Why did he let you go, do you suppose?"

"I don't know."

She looked into René's steady grey eyes, and suddenly they both knew. It was René who put it into words. "He wants something. He didn't do it for nothing, that's for sure. But what?"

Mélanie stared unseeing into space. Her mind refused to contemplate what it might be.

Twenty-four hours later, she knew what it was. A boy, in short pants, sweater, and a béret, walked up the stairs and accosted Luc. "I want to speak to your leader," he said.

Luc called René. At the approach of the newcomer, all the children gathered round.

"What is it?" René asked the stranger.

"Dujardin wants to see the girl. That one," he said, pointing to Mélanie, who remembered him as one of the boys who had blocked the sentry-box.

"What for?" René asked.

"Don't know."

"If we don't send her, then what?" René persisted.

"You'll be raided," the boy answered.

"Tell Dujardin we'll let him know at four o'clock. She'll meet him by the boat cart."

The boy turned, ran down the steps and vanished. René and Mélanie exchanged a glance.

"So, it's you he wants!"

Mélanie was too stunned to answer. The small circle of children appeared equally appalled and, like respectful spectators at a bereavement, they fell silent. One of the boys, Henri, was the first to break the spell. "Perhaps he'll settle for something else."

"Like what?" René frowned.

"Like a piece of our territory."

"We haven't got much as it is. Just from here to the other side of the stairs."

"What does he want Mélanie for?" Luc asked.

"Who knows?" René looked angrily down at his shoes, as if suspecting them of withholding knowledge from him.

There was another lengthy silence. Mélanie's mind was a blank. All thoughts were crowded out by a picture of a hard-eyed boy, a ring of black about his lips. René, who had been beating his brow with his fist, suddenly blurted out, "I've got an idea! *I'll* meet Dujardin by the boat cart. I'll make him tell me exactly what he wants from Mélanie. If he refuses or drives too hard a bargain, I'll tell him that we'll call the guards."

Calling the guards was breaking the code of the Gardens, but it had been done from time to time when one group of children seriously endangered another, so that as a threat it always carried weight.

René's plan was unanimously accepted, and at four o'clock he set off on his mission. Fifteen minutes later he was back. Mélanie was waiting for him, but his set, serious face was not an easy one to read.

"Call everybody," he ordered.

When all the children had assembled, René explained, "He's taken a fancy to Mélanie. He's not particularly interested in our territory, as long as we keep our mouths shut. If Mélanie will spend half an hour with him every day, he'll not only leave us alone, but he'll see to it that no other gang bothers us. No more raids, no more thefts, no nothing."

René looked at Mélanie. Her vision blurred, her head swam. She could not speak.

"He promises not to hurt you, though he may ask you to hold his hand. And he has sworn not to keep you more than thirty minutes."

René obviously thought she should go. Mélanie was determined not to give in to tears. By keeping silent, she might be able to hold them back.

"No raids, no nothing, that's something to consider," Henri said, as though thinking aloud. "And half an hour is not very long, is it?"

"I'll go with her," Luc offered.

"No, you can't do that," René said gruffly. "She's got to go alone. That's the deal."

"All right. I'll go." She could speak now. She was not going to cry after all.

"Good. He wants you to meet him by the pond tomorrow at three o'clock." After a pause, René continued, "Henri and I will watch you from a distance to see that he keeps his word."

As Luc showed signs of agitation, he added, "Yes, you, too, if you like."

"All right," Mélanie agreed.

Tomorrow was a long time off. Perhaps it would never come. Or Dujardin might change his mind. She would try not to think about it. She looked to where Brigitte was sitting and saw her bent over a book, her legs crossed, her head bowed, a small, slim stooped figure, as unarresting as a furled flag. Nearby, Claude was attempting somersaults. On the brink of victory, he cried out, "Brigitte, *regardes!*"

The young woman looked up, smiled in a state of trance, then bent her head again to find her lost place on the page. Mélanie walked up to her brother.

"*Regardes*, Méli!" he shouted breathlessly, undismayed by the shift in audience.

"Wonderful," Mélanie assured him, before looking about for Toinon. She spotted her sister helping another girl draw careful circles in the gravel with the leg of a folded chair, in preparation for a game of hopscotch.

Toinon had listened to René and the older children discussing Dujardin's proposition, but since the issues involved were not directly applicable to her, and did not require her active participation, she had resumed her play, her mind untouched and only momentarily deflected from its original purpose.

Claude renewed his plea for attention by calling in a wounded tone: "Méli, do look! I'm going to do it again."

And Mélanie smiled as he half-turned and landed softly on his side.

The following afternoon at three o'clock Mélanie walked down the terrace stairs. Dujardin, one foot braced against the stone edge of the pond, was waiting for her. He made no move to come forward. As he stood motionless, she noted anew his thin, colourless hair, his moist, squat hands, the black sticky

smear on his face; and a shudder ran through her. When they
had come face to face, she wondered what she was expected to
say, but the boy spoke first. "*Bonjour.* You're on time." He
nodded towards the clock on the Medici Palace, then added
unnecessarily, "We have half an hour."

If he had said eternity, Mélanie could not have felt more
oppressively gripped by time.

"Let's walk around the pond," he suggested.

Before setting off, she glanced quickly to her left. Between the
stone mouldings of the terrace, Luc's tense face was watching
her. At the foot of the stairs, René was pretending to tie his
shoe. She felt reassured.

"What's your name?" she asked.

"Dujardin."

"I know. I mean your first name?"

"I don't use it."

They walked once around the pond, and neither spoke again.

"Once more," the boy said.

At the end of the second round he explained, "I want to be where everybody can see us."

"Why?"

"I want to show you off."

"Why?"

"I bought you, didn't I?" He let out a hideously rasping laugh. "I swapped you for an armistice, didn't I?"

She braced herself for the second outburst, but the effect was the same, and she could not refrain from stepping back in recoil.

"Liquorice?"

She shook her head at the sight of the chewed-up ribbon.

"We have twelve minutes," he announced, as they were walking around the pond for the fourth time. "Want a donkey ride?"

"No, thank you."

"I've got money, you know. Plenty."

"No, thanks," she said again.

"Well, I'll buy you something sometime," he said.

"I don't want anything, thank you."

"If I want to give you something, I'll give you something."

"Yes," she whispered uncertainly.

They were silent awhile.

"Nice coat you have. Your parents fix you up good!" A little later he added, "You smell nice, too."

Mélanie saw no need to reply. Her mind was concerned with

the progress of the two hands on the palace clock. When they finally drew a right angle, it was again Dujardin who spoke first. "Go now. And mind you be here at three tomorrow."

She ran as fast as her feet would carry her.

"Well?" René greeted her. "Are you all right?"

"Yes," she said weakly. "But he doesn't wash."

René grinned. "If that's the worst thing you can say about him, we're in luck."

Mélanie did not answer. If there was any humour in the remark, it escaped her. She did not want to talk about Dujardin just then. She went over to where Brigitte was sitting and pulled up a chair. The young woman looked up from her book. "Having a good time?"

"Yes, thank you."

Before Brigitte could reimmerse herself in her novel, Mélanie asked, "What are you reading?"

"A novel."

"I know. About what?"

"Oh, it's quite thrilling. It's the story of an Arab chieftain who steals another man's wife for his harem, then when . . ."

"Does he eat liquorice?"

"Who?"

"The Arab?"

Brigitte's eyes opened wide. "Are you crazy? Who said anything about liquorice?"

Mélanie rose without a word. At the head of the stairs Louise was skipping with a rope. Mélanie went up to her. "May I jump with you?"

"Of course. I'll count to three, then you come in."

As the girls hopped up and down together, counting, "*Et six, et sept et huit* . . ." Mélanie felt better.

That night as she was about to go to bed, Luc put his arms around her. "Are you all right, Méli?"

"Yes, yes, I'm all right." And for a few minutes they stood in the doorway, their arms about each other.

The next day Mélanie found herself once again going round and round the pond with Dujardin.

"I want everybody to know you're my girl," he said.

"Oh, no!"

"Oh, yes. I've already passed the word around. I want all the gangs to know I got you."

Mélanie unconsciously brought her hand to her heart. "Oh, no!" she gasped.

"Oh yes. Just imagine a man like me getting a girl like you. That'll give them all something to talk about!"

Mélanie wished he would not laugh as if his windpipe were lined with broken glass.

"Hold my hand," he ordered.

"No, thank you."

"C'mon. Hurry."

"Not that one," she pleaded.

He looked down at the palm of his hand. It was streaked with liquorice. He turned his other hand over. It was black, matching the tips of his nails, but it was virgin of goo. "This one?" he asked.

She nodded. He walked around her to the other side. "Let's go," he urged. "We only have ten minutes."

Mélanie looked neither to the right nor to the left. She did not want to meet the eyes of anyone she knew. She composed a silent prayer: "Sainte Marie, protect me and watch over me that no one may see me. Not Maman or Papa. Not Amaury. Not Grande-Tante. Oh, and not Nicholas! Not the Fishers. Not Brigitte. Nor Joël, he would just die. Not Tante Hélène and Oncle Paul. Not Françoise, it would take so long to explain to her. Not anyone, now or ever. Amen."

She kept her eyes down, and her thoughts strayed to Jacques and M. l'Ingénieur and how they would have known what to do. They might even have chased Dujardin and his gang out of the park, running after them down the Boulevard St. Michel until they had chased them far far away, up a dark and narrow side street. She was awakened from this comforting fantasy by her companion's voice.

"*Files donc!*" he ordered. "Be here tomorrow."

As she ran off, she heard him bellow, "And don't think I'm going to wash my hands just for you!"

By the end of the week Mélanie had found out several things about Dujardin. His parents managed a small bakery. He helped them for a few hours in the evening; the rest of the time he was on his own. He knew something about almost everyone who frequented the Luxembourg. He kept a list of children who were an easy prey to thefts, and he knew which guards noticed things and which did not. In the rear of an empty shop near his home, his gang stored their spoils. Someday they would sell them. When he grew up he planned to join the Foreign Legion. "I'm afraid of nobody," was his favourite refrain.

One afternoon Mélanie came to meet him, wearing her white gloves.

"What are those for?" were his first words.

"I'm wearing them," she said, "because I can't stand that sticky stuff on your hands any longer."

"Is that so?" he sputtered. "Well, we'll take care of that!" and, taking hold of her gloved hand, he slapped the roll of liquorice into it.

"There!" he yelled, "Mlle Chichi!"

"If you don't like me," she said, feeling her advantage, "I can go." Then she lifted her hand and hurled the candy roll into the pond. She watched the widening ring that marked its descent with unrestrained delight.

"*Salaude!*" Dujardin screamed at her.

"*Au revoir,*" she waved, impressed with her own aplomb.

"Come back here! We have eight minutes yet."

She went back quietly and they followed the same old circular route without speaking. When it came time for them to part, Dujardin made a declaration: "Nobody, but nobody, is too good for me!"

But the next day he had washed his hands.

Mélanie's afternoons were now so clouded over by the dread she experienced before each tour of duty with Dujardin or by its agitated aftermath that she was almost unaware of her sister's and brothers' existence. Even when she joined her friends in a game, her mind was so abstracted that she had no more sense of their reality than if they had been ghosts.

So when Luc ran up to meet her one afternoon at half past three and said, "I have something to tell you about Brigitte," she was hardly conscious of having been addressed.

She was thinking about Dujardin and how he had suddenly grabbed her and tried to kiss her. At the approach of those red lips draped in black, she had mercilessly pummelled his stomach with her clenched hands.

"I don't want to see you ever again!" she had screamed.

Dujardin's face had twisted into a grimace. "Don't say that," he had growled. "I want you to like me."

Luc shook her arm. "A man sat next to Brigitte today."

The news left Mélanie unmoved.

"Méli, don't you remember M. Durand?"

"Of course I do."

"Well, I think we have another one."

Mélanie brushed past her brother. "Don't be silly," she said.

But Luc was right. The man came again that week and again the following week. He was under thirty, short, well built, with cauliflower ears, framing the squareness of his clean-shaven face.

"His name is Martial," Brigitte giggled. "He's a fireman. That should please you, Luc. Someday he'll take us to see the firemen in training. He's an instructor, you know."

That settled it for Luc; Martial was all right. In time his sisters came to agree with him. They all went to the firehouse and watched Martial, in what looked like long white underwear, hurl himself from the roof and land, smiling, into a sail-cloth net. They watched him vault over a wall, followed by a dozen other men in underwear and stood in awe while he slid down a pole. The climax came when Luc and Claude were taken out for a ride, grinning ecstatically from the front seat of a bright red engine.

Martial had many talents. Not only could he lift Brigitte way up in the air while she kicked her heels in protest, but he could stand still, his hands on his knees, for fifteen minutes at a stretch as one child after another jumped over his back. He never came to the park without an open paper bag filled with peanuts, hot chestnuts, or nougats. Even when he was kissing Brigitte, he never sent a child away or seemed to mind an interruption. Bidding Brigitte goodbye by the park gate, he sometimes pinched her cheek and said, "Those four kids of ours, don't you think they take after me rather than you?"

Brigitte would giggle, "Oh, you're such a tease!" But the children did not mind.

As time passed, however, and Martial's visits became more frequent, his moments spent with his arms around Brigitte lasted longer, so that he was not as much fun as he once had been.

Mélanie, meanwhile, was suffering inner disquietude and had begun to question the validity of her daily sacrifice. Whenever she approached René with the suggestion that he should break his pledge to Dujardin, she was met with a frown and a negative toss of the head. René contented himself with reminding her of the peace and freedom they had gained, and, patting her on the back, he merely said, "Oh, come, Mélanie, it's not so bad. You know you can wind him round your little finger."

It was no use. She must keep her own counsel. There was no one to whom she could confide the dreariness of those walks around the pond, the misery of her hand lying tense and uncomfortable in the boy's clumsy paw, the tautness at the pit of her stomach as she listened to his endless plans for future success and supremacy, the agony her mind underwent as she tried to think of something to say to him which would neither divulge too much about herself or her family nor in any way furnish advantageous information about her friends.

Even though Dujardin himself got bored now and then and let her off early, he seemed possessively proud of her and, he was, ironically enough, the only one who understood the full measure of her self-denial.

"You're quite a girl," he would say. "You stick to your word." Or, he would tell her, "You've got nerve. I like that."

But, to Mélanie this was painfully insufficient comfort. She wanted release from the contract. She yearned to be free, to have the hours to herself again, to be her own master. She tried on several occasions to strike some kind of bargain with Dujardin, but when she brought up her release as part of the terms, he shook his head violently from side to side. "*Ça, jamais*. Nobody is going to say that Dujardin couldn't hold on to his girl."

Whenever he said, "my girl," Mélanie felt her inner box press down more heavily against her chest. She recalled the silent compact between herself and Amaury and she wondered at the impossibility of steering one's own course, for fate had taken on an unshakable weight. From others, from the outside world, from forces beyond her control, pressures bore down on her.

When could her heart speak for itself? When would she chart her own course? It was her Garden self, her part-of-a-group self which had a relationship with Dujardin. In his presence she could not bear to think of her other selves; the one who was in love with Nicholas, or the one who was secretly engaged. She put the thought of Amaury aside, fearing that Dujardin's proximity might in some way mar the purity of their friendship. She could only keep in touch with her other selves from the outer radius of her soul.

Toinon and Mélanie were lying in their beds, wide awake. They had been too dazzled by the appearance of their father and mother in evening clothes to want to go to sleep. Accustomed as they were to seeing their parents in formal dress, they never tired of the fashion show which was part of the goodnight ritual. Mme Abbot, in a white evening gown, emeralds dangling from her ears, had, at the insistence of her children, patiently turned round several times before putting on her green silk cloak; and M. Abbot, in white tie and tails, medals pinned to his chest, had brought in his high hat still folded for Luc to spring open. Then, preparing a regal exit, they had both bowed before their wide-eyed, admiring offspring.

The two sisters were still rehearsing the scene in their minds, when there was a knock on the door and Joël walked in.

"*Holà*, Méli, Toinon, there's a party in the kitchen!"

Mélanie threw her covers off and jumped out of bed. Toinon, sleepily, followed suit. Luc appeared in the doorway to see what the commotion was about. On learning of the party downstairs, he hurried back into his room and shook Claude awake. Mélanie knotted the cord of her bathrobe, then quickly passed a comb first through her own hair, then through Toinon's.

"Ready?" Joël inquired, when the four children emerged into the hall. He picked up Claude, who was still half-asleep, and led the way to the kitchen. At the foot of the stairs, the children gasped. The ceiling in the servants' dining-room was hung with paper lanterns, candles flickered on the table and the sound of a gramophone blared forth from the kitchen, where they could see couples dancing. Brigitte whirled past with Martial, Jeanne was in the arms of a uniformed fireman, while Mme Babette's son danced with his wife. Another fireman, his gold helmet shining in the candlelight, was leaning against the stove, a glass of wine in his hand. The children were spellbound.

"We have news for you," Mme Babette greeted them, but her words were lost in the din. She raised her voice. "Turn off that gramophone! The children are here!"

The music suddenly stopped. Brigitte and Martial beamed from the archway. Mélanie stared at Brigitte. She was wearing a pink lace dress, cut so as to reveal the gentle swell of her small breasts. Mélanie had never seen her like this, with rouge on her lips and cheeks, and her small feet teetering on high-heeled shoes.

"You're so pretty," was all she could say, aware of having stared too long.

Brigitte giggled, then leant down to kiss her. Luc made his way to the stove where the helmeted fireman still stood, while Martial whirled Toinon about the room. Joël, still carrying Claude, let himself down into the only arm-chair. "Well, tell the children," he urged Mme Babette.

The cook slipped an arm about Brigitte's waist. "Well, children," she said, "Brigitte and Martial are getting married the week after next!" She waited until this intelligence sank in, then she added, "This is their engagement party."

The children were so unprepared for this that they did not know what to say. Somewhere in the back of her mind, Mélanie had expected Martial to appear someday in the park for a sharp talking-to by Mme Abbot, and Brigitte to walk out of their lives as mysteriously as Nurse had done. She was the first to rally. "Martial, congratulations!"

"Well, it's about time," the beaming fiancé retorted. "Come on, let's celebrate!"

"Shall I give the children a bit of wine?" Mme Babette asked.

"They shouldn't," Brigitte said. "But then this is a special occasion."

The cook poured a few drops of wine into four glasses.

"*À votre santé!*" Joël raised his glass from the depth of the arm-chair.

Everyone rose. "*Au bonheur! À votre santé!*" The engaged pair looked appropriately demure, as they were being toasted. The cook's son wound up the gramophone, and the dancing began again. Mélanie sat down on the arm of the chauffeur's chair.

"Claude's almost asleep," Joël said, pointing with his chin to the child curled in his arms. "In another ten minutes you had better all go back to bed."

Mélanie was silent awhile, pondering a set of questions, and finally she asked, "Will Brigitte stay with us?"

"No. She's going to keep house for Martial."

"Does Maman know?"

"She does."

She hesitated a moment before framing her next question. "Who is going to take care of us?"

"Madame will have to find somebody, of course, but perhaps not right away. After all, we'll be going to Kerouan soon."

"Then who will spend the summer with us?"

"I have a hunch that it is going to be your tutor," he said, smiling.

They both liked Mlle Denis: Mélanie, because she treated her like a grown-up person, and Joël because, as he had often remarked, she had class.

145

"But meanwhile," Mélanie persisted. Thoughts of the Luxembourg Gardens were troubling her.

"Well, Brigitte will be with you for another two weeks, then it will be time to start packing for Le Roc."

Mélanie looked down into the chauffeur's eyes and, before she quite knew what she was doing, she blurted out all about Dujardin. She had not intended to say a word to anyone, but the prospect of all those half-hours yet to be spent in the boy's company now seemed intolerable. When she stopped speaking, Joël said, "I'm glad you told me. I'll speak to Brigitte in the morning."

"But what can she do?"

"She can take you to another part of the park."

"But what about René and the other children?"

"Well, either they move, too, or they'll have to stand up to that hoodlum. The situation has gone on long enough."

It was with lighter spirits that Mélanie went back to bed some minutes later.

But by morning she felt a twinge of shame. In confiding to Joël she had betrayed the code of the Gardens, which did not allow for adult intercession. After all, René was in charge, and it was her duty to abide by his decisions. She had given in to fear and self-pity, like a coward. Mlle Denis had not yet arrived for her daily tutoring. There might still be time to set things right. Mélanie raced down to the garage. Joël was not there. She raced upstairs again. She found Brigitte making up Toinon's bed.

"Brigitte," she stammered, "it's all right about Dujardin. We'll go back as usual. You can forget about it."

"What *are* you talking about?" Brigitte seemed so genuinely bewildered that Mélanie hastily added, "Didn't Joël tell you this morning?"

"Joël? No. About what?"

"Never mind." She slammed the door, but not fast enough to miss Brigitte's pronouncement: "There are times, Mélanie, when you make no more sense than a lunatic!"

But Mélanie had also heard the ring of the doorbell. She hurried into the library, where she slipped noisily late into her chair, between Luc and Toinon, who sat, erect and affectedly studious, before a mound of notebooks.

That afternoon, as Brigitte was heading for her favourite chair, Mélanie noticed that René was sitting, seemingly relaxed, on his wooden crate, surveying his domain with a rare grin on his face. Mélanie waved to him, feeling virtuous and at ease now that her secret had not leaked out beyond Joël. René waved back, then ran to meet her. Before he had quite reached her, he shouted: "He's gone!"

Mélanie said, "Who?", but she already knew. There was only one person for whom the pronoun served as ample identification, so constantly was he on their minds.

"Dujardin, of course," René said, smiling expansively. "He stole a woman's purse this morning. She called the guard. He, in turn, whistled for his *confrères*. There was a merry chase. It must have been magnificent! I wish I'd been there to see it."

"Was he caught?"

"No, he got away. But there is no sign of him today."

Mélanie let out a sigh of relief. She was glad Dujardin had escaped. Foe though he was, he was none the less a child and, as such, he belonged to her world; and it was only right that he had outwitted the law, the grown-up world. If justice was to be meted out to him, it would have to come from his contemporaries, from the children he had terrorized in the park.

"How about *les Jardiniers*?" Luc broke in.

"They're nowhere to be seen. They'll have to lie low for awhile. Dujardin won't dare show his face for some time."

Mélanie felt suddenly weak. That this news affected her directly had just begun to dawn on her. No more tours about the pond. Not her own manoeuvring, but fate had granted her an unexpected reprieve.

"We are free! Free! Free!" René burst out exuberantly. "The place is ours! I've been waiting for you Abbots to start a game of hide-and-seek." He ran off, weaving like a drunkard, to collect his gang. He pulled children by the sleeve, calling, "We are free! Free! Free!"

Mélanie had never before seen so disorganized and jubilant a game of hide-and-seek as followed. Not only did every child run out of bounds, but there was so much noise and unrestrained giggling that no hiding place was safe.

Three o'clock struck and Mélanie did not even glance in the direction of the pond.

She was resting on a bench, when René suddenly came up behind her.

"Well," he said. "How does it feel?"

"Like Easter," she said.

René walked around the bench and sat down beside her. He took her hand and shook it. "*Vive la liberté!*" he said.

"*Vive la liberté!*" she replied. And they both burst out laughing.

ON THAT TERRIBLE DAY, MME ABBOT HAD come smiling into the nursery, with a letter in her hand.

"I have a letter from Nicholas," she announced to her children. "I thought you would like to hear how well he is doing. It's from Vienna, where he has had a most successful concert. He is spending his honeymoon there. But I'll read it to you."

The word her mother had just spoken startled Mélanie into total immobility. Surely she had not heard right. Mme Abbot began to read: "Dear Abbots, I should have written long before this to bring you up to date on my news—all of it good, you will be glad to know. In fact, good fortune has been trailing me —or should I say preceding me—ever since I started on this concert tour. To show you how well received I have been in London, Munich and here, in Vienna, I enclose the reviews. They praise my technique, as you can see, but they seem to feel that I lack a certain maturity of feeling. Well, there should be changes in that quarter soon. You see, I married Elisabeth three weeks ago. When I first told you about her, I know how concerned you both were over her recent marital failure. Such an intensely personal matter sounds cold in conversation or on paper, but when you meet her your doubts, I know, will vanish. Young as she is, she is none the less wise and selfless—and, of course, her knowledge of music is invaluable to me. But what I know is even closer to your hearts—we are in love, deeply, truly, maturely. We shall be returning to Paris on the 17th. I'll telephone you—and may the proud bridegroom present his new bride? As always, gratefully and affectionately, Nicholas."

Mme Abbot folded the letter. "Well, isn't this good news?"

Mélanie gazed at her, unseeing. If her mother had taken a small knife and herself thrust it into her daughter's back, Mélanie could not have felt more stunned or more betrayed. Was it really possible that she did not know?

Mother and daughter stared at one another. When Mme Abbot asked, "Child, what's the matter?" Mélanie turned and fled from the nursery. She ran down the hall to the bedroom and pulled the door wide open. Brigitte, who was standing amid a pile of soiled linen and counting out loud, looked at her surprised.

Mélanie slammed the door shut and continued to race down the corridor. She flew down the stairs, past the kitchen, and into the courtyard. She stopped in an effort to check her uncontrollable sobs, then ran, as though pursued, into the garage and fell on her face in the back seat of the car. Joël, who was half-hidden below the upright bonnet, raised his head, then, after a moment, lowered it again and went on listening to the gentle purring of the engine.

Mélanie felt a wild disorder in her brain. How could her mother have inflicted this sharp pain into her unsuspecting heart, pricking her balloon of hopes and dreams and leaving her defenceless before the wounds of love? That Nicholas had hardly noticed her mute advances, Mélanie well knew. But he was a dedicated man, engrossed in his music. She had never imagined that he might have had a life outside of her own living-room, where his need was known and would be answered. She felt a lance pierce through her heart—a lance twenty years long.

She half-rose on the seat cushion.

"Joël?"

The chauffeur's head emerged from below the bonnet. "Yes?"

"I ... I ..." but she could not go on.

Joël came nearer, but when he bent over the back seat as if to pick her up, she pushed him away. She was now a new person, a creature utterly alone, a woman with a broken heart. And she cried as none of her selves had ever cried before.

After a while she looked up. The chauffeur was still standing by the car door.

"Joël?"

"Yes."

"He's married."

"Who?"

"Nicholas."

"I see."

Her sobs had subsided, but her limbs seemed made of grass. Joël climbed into the back seat. His bulk shook the whole rear of the car.

"Joël . . ."

"Don't talk," he admonished. After a long pause, he said, "The world hasn't really come to an end, *mon enfant*. Tomorrow is another day. And tomorrow I shall be driving you to Brigitte's wedding. Then before you know it, we'll be in Kerouan. All your friends will be there, Amau . . ."

Mélanie turned and pounded him with her fists. The world *had* come to an end.

"No . . . No . . . !" she cried.

"Hey, there!" he said, grabbing hold of both her wrists.

Something terrible was happening inside her. She fell with her face across the chauffeur's knees. A moan issued from her throat, as she felt her box spring open and saw a myriad blurred images dance before her eyes. She wanted to call out, to Joël, to her mother, but she was utterly voiceless and without breath.

MÉLANIE WAS SITTING ON THE STONE RIM of the pond while Dujardin raged before her. He had returned that morning from his week of exile, a grin of triumph on his face, and once again *les Jardiniers* could be seen strutting confidently about the park.

It was a hot June afternoon. Huge shadows stretched across the hard ground and the still water of the pond. Children running past raised a trail of dust where not long before all had been mud and sodden earth; even the clouds gliding lazily beneath the sky seemed crisp and dry. But Mélanie was only aware of the unseasonable heat burrowing itself into the small of her back and of the strange new weight within her. She sat, listless and unseeing, as Dujardin hopped up and down in a paroxysm of anger. He was screaming at her, telling her that she could not go, that he would not let her go to Brittany. Then suddenly his voice sank to a whisper, and, cajoling, he offered to bring her cakes from his parents' bakery if only she would remain in Paris for the summer. But neither his threats nor his promises had the power to move her.

When he had come looking for her earlier that afternoon, she had been surprised to find that he no longer frightened her. On the contrary, he appeared to have shrunk to a pathetic size, and his uncouthness had stirred her to genuine pity. She could almost believe that she had towered above him, for the weight of her secret seemed not only to have given her strength, but height as well. The secret she carried was a pain in the region of her heart, a cumbersome, indefinable pain that was like no other she had experienced. It was so real, so immediate that it had displaced her box. She could not now remember what joys and fears her box had once held. She was a person who had been where no child she knew had been, to a land unknown to Dujardin, unknown to her friends in the Luxembourg Gardens.

She thought of Françoise who was quiet and grown-up, and she had a great longing to see her. She would have lots of things to tell her when they met again in Kerouan, though she was not sure whether she would mention the piano which would now be still for ever, or try to explain why she had not gone into the living-room to look at it. Yet Françoise might guess, for she was wise. Mélanie recalled how the previous summer her friend had often lain, serious and still on the sand, pondering mysterious thoughts while gazing at the sun through her dark glasses. Even the little children playing nearby had sensed and respected her wisdom. Françoise never fussed with them when they argued over which pail belonged to whom or whether or not a whelk was dead in its shell, but when they became really angry with each other, because in their ignorance and perplexity they could not arrive at a conclusion, she would rise slowly and, in a firm but gentle voice, would say: "The whelk is dead," or "This pail belongs to Monique." Immediately the children's baffled anger died away and, after the sea snail had been thrown out or the pail returned, they went back to their games, not thanking Françoise but trusting her. They believed her because she, too, carried a secret, and no one knew what it was, not even Mélanie.

Dujardin, his arms flailing the air, his face grimacing with frustration, was still venting his wrath. Mélanie looked at him a moment then stood up and started to walk away. She was stopped by his wounded cry: "Where are you going?"

"I am going up to the terrace," she said. "And tomorrow I'm leaving for Kerouan, because there is no changing things."

She turned to face the boy who was staring at her, his body still as stone, his mouth agape with surprise. Then she waved, saying, "Have a nice summer," and, not hurrying, she reached the terrace stairs.

She walked past René who was pitching his knife into the bark of a tree, past Luc and Toinon who were racing their scooters, past Mademoiselle Denis, now occupying Brigitte's favourite chair, and sat down on an empty bench. She wanted to tend her secret and reflect on her new self. But Claude, who had been making a design of stones on the ground, spotted her and, running up, called, "Look, Méli! I found a jewel!"

She bent over his extended palm. "That's nice . . ." she said, then caught herself. She cast a quick glance at her brother's open face and hesitated. Then, with resolution in her voice, she added, "But it's not a jewel, Claude, it's a piece of broken glass," and rising again, Mélanie walked over to the terrace wall. Shading her eyes, she looked down at the pond. Dujardin had gone. The children pushing their toy sailboats across the water looked small and far away.